She walked through the summer wood, searching for what had been hidden one hundred years before she was born.

First of all, her gloves were too big. Here she was, having embarked upon her first solo research assignment, and she'd had to borrow gloves from one of the locals. She could almost hear her old prof, Magnelli, chiding her for the rookie lapse.

Secondly, every tree in this forest west of Colorado Springs, every single damn tree in all the Rocky Mountains, looked the same as the last.

She stopped, removed her ball cap, and wiped her forehead on her sleeve in a manner she knew was unladylike. If a woman's manners fell off in the woods and no one was around to hear, would they make a sound?

"Miss Emily?"

So much for being alone.

Praise for Lance Hawvermale

"Deftly written, [Hawvermale's] debut is full of appealing characters and moments that sparkle with tenderness."

~Publisher's Weekly

~*~

"[Hawvermale] pushes the envelope, taking the commonplace theme of women's friendships into dangerous territory and dramatizing what women can do not just to help themselves, but also to bring justice to others."

~Booklist

~*~

"Hawvermale, balancing suspense with character study, includes enough pauses between the adrenaline-pumping scenes to give his leads the time they need to grow."

~Kirkus Reviews

~*~

"Hawvermale expertly weaves complex characters and secrets, luring you from one chapter to the next. His prose is at the same time smooth and riveting."

~Jean Rabe, author

The Echo Holders

by

Lance Hawvermale

The Echo Holders

Cover Art by *Abigail Owen*

The Wild Rose Press, Inc.
PO Box 708
Adams Basin, NY 14410-0708
Visit us at www.thewildrosepress.com

Publishing History
First Mainstream Mystery Rose Edition, 2019
Print ISBN 978-1-5092-2448-7
Digital ISBN 978-1-5092-2449-4

Published in the United States of America

Dedication

To Amelia, who changed everything

Chapter One

She walked through the summer wood, searching for what had been hidden one hundred years before she was born.

First of all, her gloves were too big. Here she was, having embarked upon her first solo research assignment, and she'd had to borrow gloves from one of the locals. She could almost hear her old prof, Magnelli, chiding her for the rookie lapse.

Secondly, every tree in this forest west of Colorado Springs, every single damn tree in all the Rocky Mountains, looked the same as the last.

She stopped, removed her ball cap, and wiped her forehead on her sleeve in a manner she knew was unladylike. If a woman's manners fell off in the woods and no one was around to hear, would they make a sound?

"Miss Emily?"

So much for being alone. She turned toward her driver, whom she'd asked to wait for her at the truck. "What do you need, Tunny?"

The big man screwed up his face in a look of worry. "Just wanted to make sure you ain't lost."

Emily smiled faintly. " I'm just trying to get the lay of the land. I'm not ready for a full-blown exploration at this point, so I don't need a bodyguard. Why don't you go back to the truck, okay?"

"You sure?"

"Tunny, please."

With a shrug of his mountainous shoulders, Tunny left her, moving like she suspected Sasquatch moved, heavy and agile at the same time. Soon his footfalls faded.

Which left Emily alone with the trees that held the secret of the ages.

Carefully she moved from one to the next, searching the bark around their bases, ever hopeful, the way the mourning dove is always certain of the dawn.

****

That night, Emily conducted a scholarly investigation of the populace in the place where every good anthropologist begins: the local bar.

A butt occupied every booth at the Cross Cut. She sat on a stool near the ladies room—always a strategic position—Tunny on her left and another new friend, Raspberry Rono, on her right. A sixteen-point antler rack shared space on the wall with what must have been taxidermist's humor—a stuffed two-headed bass. Emily had never been much for socializing and even less for alcohol, but the big three-oh must have loosened some of her springs. The day after her birthday, she was actually talking to these people instead of retreating into her introverted shell like the hermit crab she was.

"So how long do you think it'll take you to find it?" the bartender asked.

"There's no time line on things like this," Emily said.

"Things like what, exactly?"

"Research."

"Ah" Apparently satisfied, he left to tend to a

thirsty customer.

On the juke, a country crooner sang about digging up bones. Emily found that fairly close to the mark, considering what she'd come to rural Colorado to do.

"So what's the plan for findin' something out there in the woods?" Tunny wanted to know. He was working on his third beer but showed no effects. By the looks of him, he could have thumb-wrestled Paul Bunyan into submission, so Emily figured it would take more than three beers to slow him down.

"I'll explain it in the morning," she assured him.

"So there is, uh, a real plan then?"

Emily moved her tongue around the inside of her cheek, wondering how to respond. The doubt on Tunny's face showed as readily as if an inept artist had painted it there. The esteemed Frank Magnelli, acclaimed anthropology professor, already warned her that many would view her work as having no academic worth, so her bodyguard's lack of faith didn't gall her. She was just about to say something she'd probably regret when Raspberry intervened.

"Listen up, cuz," Rono said, elbows on the bar, "as I'm only gonna say this one time." He smacked his lips dramatically. "Knew a man one time, name of Bojangles. And damned if that cat didn't dance for me. Old Bojangles be many a thing, a wise man among them. Said to me one day, 'Rono my boy, don't you ever, and I mean *never,* call into question a woman's plans, especially not on a night when she's buying the brew.'"

With that, he knocked back the last two swallows of his own.

Emily smiled. "I guess that means I'm buying."

Rono grinned so wide all his teeth showed in his wizened face. " "Thought you'd never ask."

Things went easier after that. She got to know these men a bit better, which was good, considering they were serving as her guides. Occasionally one of the locals approached and introduced themselves, as any new addition to a town of eleven-hundred was bound to draw attention. They all seemed downright pleased to meet her, and no one quizzed her too intimately on the nature of her work. Nor did anyone opine she was insane.

Then why do you feel that way? Magnelli's voice asked inside her head.

As she had no answer for him, she shut him down by ordering another beer.

Chapter Two

Across the room, the money piled up.

Between the empty bottles liberally lined up on the loggers' table lay a hundred and ninety dollars, give or take, the largest pot of the night. The Cross Cut was no Vegas poker den, so the stakes were lower, but the game no less intense. For the most part, the players spoke only among themselves, not distracted by the music or the gentle mayhem of this Saturday night.

These were timber-men, some generations deep. *Lumberjacks*, they were called by those outside the trade. They knew the wood and smelled of it, a subtle cologne of soil and green, growing things.

They grew quietly drunk.

"I'm not sure of my math anymore," Hartlet admitted, peering again at the corner of his cards, that vital place where suit and number were marked. "What are the odds of me pulling a flush?"

"'Bout as good as the odds of Charley findin' a woman who'll put up with him," MacGregor said.

Nobody laughed. They were too intent. Sometimes they were wild and sometimes—like tonight—they felt the seriousness of the earth in their bones.

Charley tossed his cards away. "Looks like I fold. Either that or I won't have money left for gas to get me home."

"Me, too," Hartlet said, tossing in his cards.

5

MacGregor scanned his hand; his broad face gave nothing away. "I'm in. Raise her up another twenty. Joseph? How about you?"

Joe spit a line of Skoal into his beer bottle. "Hell, you only live once, right?" He flicked a twenty-dollar-bill into the pot.

They all looked at the last man at the table.

He sat a bit back in his chair and every now and then rocked gently on its legs, like a man sitting on his front porch. He wore a shirt his uncle had owned in the 70s, with pearl snaps and frayed cuffs. His black hair—blacker even than the ace of spades he concealed in his hand—fell to his collar and a little past. His cheeks were smooth and well-defined, like polished stone.

"Mace?" MacGregor said. "You in?"

Mason Hitapwa pretended he didn't hear them. He had to do that sometimes, playing the inscrutable Indian so they wouldn't think he was normal. That had always been his biggest fear, to live a flatline existence, so his charade was to wrap himself in silence and let them apply to him their half-baked myths about Native Americans. He stared at his cards, his face like that of a seer, while inside he giggled like a boy about the full house he'd finally drawn.

"Mason?"

Finally he looked up.

They waited.

He thought this might be the perfect time to relate to them some philosophical bit of Hopi advice, but he couldn't think of any off-hand. Of course, he could have quoted something from *Dances with Wolves* and they wouldn't have known the difference.

"I'm in," he said, and slid two tens into the pot.

"Call," MacGregor said quickly.

"Call," Joe added.

Mason nodded.

MacGregor laid down two pairs. Immediately he looked at Joe and Mason, searching their eyes for hints of his fate.

"Damn," Joe said and flicked his cards away. "I thought you were bluffing."

MacGregor swung his gaze at Mason. "Well?"

Mace wanted to smile but held it back. Mortgage was due and he needed that money. But enigmatic Indians didn't boast. His grandfather had advised him in the various ways to act around white men, and though Mason had more white friends than native ones, he fell back on his granddad's counsel and kept his grin tucked behind his teeth.

"Full house. Aces over fives."

MacGregor and the others groaned.

Hartlet drained his glass. "That's it for me. "Old lady's going to rip my teeth out as it is, spending her bingo money like that."

"You didn't spend it," Charley said, his face flushed a hops-induced red. "You lost it."

"Yeah, yeah. See ya tomorrow, Mace, ya lucky bastard."

"You bet, Mac."

In various states of inebriation, the men departed the table, leaving Mason alone with his winnings. He didn't want to be here when Helena, the night waitress, decided to amble over and ask where he planned to spend it. She was married and in love with everyone but her husband. So Mason folded the money semi-carefully and jammed it into his jeans pockets, then pulled his denim jacket from the back of the chair and left the table. Only a few folks said hello as he wove through the tables toward the door. That was their way with him. They thought he was a loner. Mason did nothing to change their minds.

Halfway across the room, he noticed the stranger. She sat at the bar but looked out of place there. In a town this size, you either fit in or you left people wondering. Mason was curious, but he was also eager to get out under the sky, where he always felt more at home. As he passed the jukebox, a lovesick cowboy was singing about how his baby had gotten good at goodbye. Mason was almost out the door when the bartender, Paul, called out in the middle of the song's chorus, "Listen up for a second, folks!"

The room quieted. Mason turned as Paul motioned toward the woman at the bar who looked uncomfortable at the sudden attention. "I'd like you all to meet somebody new to Rockerton.

Mason waited at the door, for no other reason than to hear her name.

Chapter Three

Later, Emily would blame what next happened on age. Surely had she not been suffering from the aftershocks of turning thirty, the earth wouldn't have moved like that beneath her, shooting her off the stool and onto both feet after the bartender introduced her.

"…let's all give her a real Rockerton howdy!" he bellowed.

Everyone cheered.

Emily blushed. At least she was still on her feet. Facing strangers had always been her weakness. They said Achilles was impervious except in that spot his mother held him when dipping him into magic waters. With Emily, someone must have been holding on to whatever part of her was connected to stage fright because nowhere else did she ever feel vulnerable.

"Thank you," she said, holding the smile in place and praying it stayed. "You're all…very kind."

"Speech!" someone yelled.

Emily forced the smile even wider. No way was she giving a monologue.

"Welcome to town!" another voice added.

"Thanks."

"Where you from?"

Emily looked in the direction from which the question had come. A group of men in trucker hats formed a crowd at the far end of the bar. She knew her answer would elicit jeers, but she couldn't think quickly enough to fire back a witty rejoinder. "I'm, uh…from New Jersey."

Their reaction didn't surprise her. They booed, albeit good-naturedly, complaining about the eastern seaboard in general and city folk in particular.

Emily felt her blush deepen as heat spread down her chest.

"Finally came to your senses and moved west, huh?" one of the men asked, loudly enough to be heard across the bar.

"Something like that."

"What kind of business you in?"

Emily wondered if all newcomers received such an introduction. Though the tavern wasn't quite filled to capacity, there were at least fifty people gathered here. She knew they meant no harm. They seemed like fine people. Had they known the extent of her discomfort, surely they wouldn't have kept her so squarely on the spot.

"I'm…a scientist," she said. Maybe *scientist* wasn't exactly the right word, but it was close enough.

"And what's your science?" one of them wanted to know. "Tunny said you were into trees. That makes you a botanist, right?"

"Well…" She shifted her feet, hoping the stool would catch her if her knees suddenly gave out. She'd never been much of a public speaker. "I'm less focused on plants, and…just on trees, really."

"So am I," said a man near the jukebox. "Focused on cuttin' them down."

That got some laughs. Emily didn't know why.

The man chugged a few more swallows from his

glass and nodded. "Yep, just cut those bastards down as fast as God can grow 'em."

Then it happened.

Later she would write it off to the stubbornness of turning thirty. "I'm here to keep them from being cut down."

The man's smile held, but it became an uncertain thing on his face. The laughter faded, and everyone looked at Emily, wondering if they'd missed the New Jersey humor.

"What do you mean?" The man's face was rough from years of working under the sun. "I ask because this town is built on the timber industry. If you know what I'm saying."

What *did* she mean? Emily was sorry the moment the words had left her mouth. The last thing she wanted was to upset a group of people she didn't even know.

A woman in the back spoke up. "You an environmentalist or something?"

"No, it's not that…I just…"

"Not to disrespect your business or anything," another one of the timber-cutters said, "but sometimes outsiders don't understand how we work. We don't do the slash-and-burn thing like them radicals in the Amazon. We plant an area after we harvest it."

"Yeah," his buddy said, "so you can turn your tree-hugging, hemp-powered car around and head back to Jersey. They have great atmosphere there, too. They call it smog."

Several in the crowd looked uneasy after this exchange; they studied the scuffs in the hardwood floor or took a sudden interest in their beer.

Emily's new friends, Tunny and Rono, sat slack-jawed on their stools, looking ashamed but also too scared to do anything about it. No Galahads here. So much for one of them coming to her rescue.

And so, perhaps for the first time in her life, Emily rescued herself. "You have no idea who I am or what I'm hoping to find out there."

She must have said it with a certain amount of steel in her voice, for the silence only hardened around her.

Knowing only a new and unfamiliar heat in her bones, she pressed on. "A dendrologist is someone who studies trees. I don't know anything about what dendrologists do or how they do it. Neither am I a botanist, not that it's any of your business." She indicted them all as she sent a glare across the room. "But if you have to label me, then I suppose I'm what you call a symbologist." She swung her gaze directly at the man who'd insulted her. "So you can turn your tree-cutting, ozone-depleting pickup truck in the direction of the library and go look that word up. They have a certain book there. They call it a dictionary."

Someone whooped in appreciation at this. A few clapped, obviously glad to see her get the best of the bully.

"My name is Emily Radsco," she announced, having never felt less Emilylike. She challenged them all, her cheeks so warm she felt aflame. "And I'm buying the next round for the house."

She could not have played it better. Nearly everyone in the place hooted or applauded in appreciation. She won them over with that, at least for now, and the room returned to its noisy, cheerful state. Rono patted her on the arm as she sank down to her stool, but she hardly felt the contact. She was too full of alcohol and excitement; it was all she could do to keep from throwing up.

Rono smiled, revealing fantastically white teeth. "Knew there was a reason I came here tonight, yessir, indeed."

"Yeah," Tunny agreed, hoisting his mug. "Free beer."

The men laughed and knocked back their brew, while between them Emily—recently thirty—sat there and waited for the world to stop spinning.

****

Outside, the Colorado night had turned into a kind of dying fire. Mason looked up at the stars and thought the air here in summertime was like the bottom of an old iron stove. Though it was cool, the promise of heat remained, waiting for its embers to be kicked awake by dawn.

Having just seen his supervisor, Larry Ellsworth, get taken to task by the woman from New Jersey, Mason was in high spirits. Men like Larry deserved an occasional public defeat. Mason passed through the parking lot, the heels of his boots a hollow cadence on the ground. An extraordinary number of insects clogged the high lamps. For a while Mason found himself fascinated by their sheer numbers and by their willingness to remain captivated by bright objects.

Fearing he might find a metaphor there, he lowered his head and walked faster.

He left the cars behind. He didn't own a vehicle. Not anymore.

Besides, things were better on foot, at least in the summer. As long as you didn't have far to go, you were always better off getting there the old-fashioned way.

"Sounds like something Jimmy would have said," Mason realized out loud. Jimmy White Cloud Hitapwa was his grandfather, font of eternal yet questionable wisdom.

Mason set off down the road. He lived a mile west from the Cross Cut and up the mountain a quarter-mile more.

Cars passed him, little more than dark shapes in the gloom. He counted his steps as he walked, reaching his age—thirty-six—before starting over again. For some reason he was afraid to count beyond that number, as if it might bring bad luck. Like that childhood superstition about stepping on a crack and breaking someone's back.

One of the cars slowed and stopped beside him. The driver's window unrolled. "Yo, Mace!"

Hands thrust in his jacket pockets, Mason ambled over to Raspberry Rono's long black Cadillac that looked not unlike a hearse.

"Though I already know your answer," Rono said, grinning in the dashboard light, "you know I'm gonna ask anyway."

Mason offered him a polite smile. "Thanks for the offer, but I'm okay."

"A nice life for a walk?"

"Something like that."

Letting the car idle in the middle of the road, Rono said, "Miss Emily, allow me the pleasure of introducing our resident Apache, Mr. Mason Hitapwa."

Ignoring the Apache remark, Mason glanced toward the passenger's seat. "Hey."

She was nearly invisible in the dark."Hello."

Mason recognized her. "The symbologist."

She might have smiled. In the dark it was hard to say. "That's right. I didn't mean to, uh, broadcast that everywhere. It just came out. Sorry."

"That's okay. Personally I've always wondered why we've never had a symbologist here in town, so I'm glad you stopped by." Pleased with his sufficiently obscure response, he backed away from the car, giving Rono a wave. The man earned the name Raspberry during his days as a knuckleball pitcher in high school, though Mason had never asked for further details. "Thanks again."

"Not a problem, *amigo*. Just trying to be the moderately good Samaritan."

The Cadillac pulled away.

Mason smiled to himself and kept walking. As he made his way down the desolate road, with deep Colorado forests on either side of him, he tried to remember what the symbologist had looked like. The light in the car had been insufficient, and the illumination in the Cross Cut hadn't been much better.

Why do you suddenly care? he asked himself. *What does it matter?*

As usual, Mason had no answer for his own questions.

Chapter Four

Emily awoke in a purple cave.

Where am I?

For several moments there was only the soft beating of her heart and—from somewhere nearby—the coy whistle of a warbler. Stuffed into her sleeping bag, she wondered for a moment if she were dreaming. She was still back in Newark, her body in her cramped apartment but her dream-self roaming the distant worlds of myth. But then the fabric above her moved, prodded by a limb, and she remembered that she was sixteen-hundred miles from home, lying on her back in an eggplant-colored tent she'd bought on sale.

She groaned and wished exquisitely for coffee.

Five minutes later she'd struggled free of her sleeping bag and tent and took her first real breath of the morning. The woods were green and complete. Everything was held in place by the invisible strings of nature, into which Emily felt like she entered, like a woman passing through cobwebs. Then it all woke up, the small animals and the bugs, the drowsy birds and leaves. Who needed coffee with a tonic like this?

"I do," she said, and fixed a pot on her portable stove.

She could have stayed in a motel. Scholars did that when traveling. But Emily wanted to immerse herself in the wilderness, hoping that proximity would convince it to release some of its secrets. Perhaps if she slept in their bosom, the forest gods would think she belonged.

Half an hour later, having brushed her teeth and washed her face with environmentally friendly products, she pulled on a light vest, tightened the laces on her recently purchased trail boots, and set off with her handbag full of divining rods.

The first rod was a surveyor's GPS device. She would use it to plot the location of her finds, if she ever made any. Just as importantly, the little computer could call up to the satellites and guide her back to camp when she inevitably got lost.

Not for the first time, she marveled at how all trees looked the same.

Known to the locals as *quakies*, the aspens were silver exclamation points, declaring the beauty of this land with beautiful insistence. Emily had spoken the truth when she claimed she was no specialist in trees, but her search for the riddles of the past had required her to learn a little Latin. Somewhere in these specimens of *Populus tremuloides* was a message left by travelers a hundred years in the past.

Emily referred to the hexagonal graph she'd drawn of the surrounding woods. After marking the first section to be investigated, she began inspecting trunks.

The white bark was clean and unmarked. Emily scanned the first tree with care, kneeling to see its base and then slowly rising to survey its height up to roughly six feet. Shaded by the large round leaves, she circled the tree, eyes crawling over every bend and contour.

Nothing.

She went to the next tree in the hex.

By yesterday's experience she knew it would take

roughly forty-five minutes to investigate each hex on her map. She certainly could have sped up the process had she enlisted a few assistants, but by doing that she'd ram right into two of her personal drawbridges. Both were usually maintained in an upright position, permitting no one to cross her moat. First and foremost, she learned early on that she functioned better alone, especially when doing research. Undergrad students had their uses, but Emily never enjoyed divvying up work just to save herself some time. Secondly, this was a holy place. And holy places had always liberated her. The effect wouldn't have been nearly as emancipating had she shared it with someone else.

She spent the afternoon drawing lines through hexes when they offered her no treasure but remaining consistently hopeful that it was all about to change.

****

The bulldozer crashed a heavy tangle of branches into the pile.

"Easy does it!" Larry yelled, waving his gloved hand. "Don't drive the damn thing like it's on fire."

Mason barely acknowledged the foreman's warning. He wore sunglasses beneath the rim of his yellow hardhat, and knew his eyes were nothing but meaningless mirrors. His grandfather would have approved. When his work was complete, he shut off the engine and climbed down from the seat.

Around him, the camp teemed with motion and noise. This was Mason's world. It was a world of buzzing. His father had framed houses for a living back in Arizona, and that was a world of banging. But in the timber trade, most noises were one octave of buzz or another. He decided that if there was a word that described his trade it was *separation.*

"I'm a separator," he said to himself, as the saws around him churned away, dividing one thing from another.

"Heads up, Mace!"

He emerged from his reverie just in time to catch a heavy clutch of keys.

"We took a vote," Larry said. "You're driving for lunch."

"I don't remember voting."

"By *we* I mean *me*. I voted. Don't drive my truck like you handle that dozer, okay? I just paid it off."

"I'll try to keep her out of the ditch." Mason briefly considered giving his boss a good-natured ribbing about his losing debate last night with the out-of-town woman. A few of the crew had made the mistake of challenging her, and she'd gotten the best of them. But Larry seemed to be in a fair mood this morning, so there was no reason to provoke him. Instead, Mason simply nodded and walked down the temporary road they'd made through the trees. He didn't mind making the run to Rockerton for sandwiches. The foreman's truck was air-conditioned, and the radio had a knack for always finding the saddest country music out of Nashville.

He tossed his hardhat onto the seat, fiddled with the radio dial, then drove down the slope, remembering his seat belt two miles later. He pulled the shoulder harness across his chest, took his eyes off the dirt trail only long enough to slot the metal tongue into the latch.

That one moment was long enough.

Chapter Five

Keeping her gaze moving from the base of one aspen to the next, Emily didn't realize she'd stepped into a clearing until she heard the truck bearing down.

She looked up. The road was little more than two tire tracks snaking through the trees. The truck absorbed all of it, a huge thing rumbling through the woods. Emily gasped; reflexes turned her away even as her mind told her that she wasn't going to make it.

How unfair, she had time to think, *to die so close to discovery*. She'd seen something imprinted on that last tree; she was certain of it.

The undergrowth snagged her foot, and she fell face-down in the dirt.

The oversized tires dug into the soil as the truck braked. The back end swung around and clipped one of the aspens. Both truck and tree reverberated from the impact, shaking loose a hundred leaves. The collision stole much of the vehicle's momentum, so that it came to a sudden stop at an angle across the road.

Emily spun, her butt on the ground, bracing herself with her hands. Her fingers gripped the dirt, chest rising and falling like a bellows, she stared through her hair at the black metal monster that just came within ten feet of killing her.

The driver swung open his door.

Emily wanted to inventory herself. Had she

sprained anything? Pulled any underused muscles? But her gaze strayed back to the tree and what she might have seen there. She'd dropped her canvas satchel when the truck appeared. Now that tired old handbag marked her point of entry into what she hoped was a forgotten world.

"Ma'am?"

She looked away from the tree.

"Are you hurt?"

Was she? She shook her head.

He came to her, lean in his jeans and denim jacket. Emily had another random thought, this one about out-of-body experiences and how they say your life passing before your eyes during moments like this. If that were the case, then Emily had seen nothing but her own hair in her face and a shitload of trees.

Now *that* was funny.

"What is it?" he asked, crouching in front of her. "What's wrong?" His hands hovered in front of him as if he wanted to check her for injuries but was afraid of getting too close.

Deciding she better say something to assure him she wasn't the madwoman he suspected her to be, she cleared her throat. "And who said research isn't dangerous work?"

He raised an eyebrow. "I'm not sure I know what that means."

"I wasn't aware there was a road out here. I didn't mean to—"

"Are you kidding me? I almost ran you over. It wasn't your fault."

She leaned to the side to get a look at his truck, winced when she saw the dent.

He glanced back. "Yeah, that one's not going to go over very well with the company. I won't exactly be bringing her back in the same condition as when I left. Are you sure you're all right?"

"Other than some dirt on my second-favorite pair of pants, I'm fine." She started to push herself up but accepted his hand when he offered. "Thanks."

He still looked like a man searching for the right apology. "I've never seen anyone out here before, so it caught me off guard when you stepped out of the trees like that. Maybe I wasn't paying enough attention."

"Don't worry about it. I said they were only my *second* favorite pair, so I don't feel the need to sue. At least not for very much."

He didn't seem to know if she were joking or not.

"What is this place, anyway?" she asked, hoping to distract him from his guilt. "I'm not from around here, but I'm *sure* this road wasn't on my map."

"Logging lane. It's only temporary. We're working a couple of miles up the hill." At that moment he recognized her. "Wait a minute. You're the symbologist."

For a moment she wondered about the fabulous efficiency of small-town gossip. Had her antics at the bar last night already climbed halfway up the mountain?. Then she realized she'd seen this man before, if only briefly. "Right. I remember. From last night. You joked about the town being in need of someone like me."

He laughed. The sudden sound startled her, the way the birds sometimes surprised her when breaking from the aspen boughs. "Yeah, it was late and my sense of humor was on its last leg. That was the best I could do." He hooked a thumb toward his truck. "Can I give you a ride? I was on my way into town for lunch."

"Appreciated but not necessary. Believe it or not, I'm working out here." She realized, then, two things about him. One, he was probably a logger who might have been responsible for mowing down some of the very trees she was trying to locate. And two, he was, as her mother would've said, as easy looking as a pie left to cool on a Sunday sill. His dark hair hung a little too close to his collar for office work, and his cheeks and chin were smoothly shaved. His cheekbones and complexion were distinctly Indian.

Not Indian, Magnelli's chiding voice reminded her, ever politic. *Native.*

Yes, Native. Whatever. His eyes were so brown as to be almost black.

She held up the hiker's GPS unit she wore on a lanyard around her neck. "I'm not as lost as it seems."

He took a step back and appraised her. "You don't seem that way at all." He smiled. "Sorry again about...well, about almost running you over."

"Your truck took more damage than I did."

"Yeah." He looked at the V-shaped dent just above the left rear wheel, then glanced back at her. "What kind of work?"

"I'm sorry?"

"You said you're working out here."

"Oh, right. Uh..." She was reluctant to reveal anything. So far she'd hadn't found anything to justify this cross-country trip. Or had she? "It's not really very interesting."

He slipped his hands into the pockets of his jeans. "Rye bread."

Emily assumed she'd misheard him. "Pardon?"

"I said rye bread. Meaning that the most interesting part of my day is going to be deciding between rye and honey wheat on my sandwich for lunch. So even if you're just out here counting the spots on monarch butterflies, I figure you've got on one me."

Yes, her mother would've loved this one. All of that and clean teeth, too.

"Don't say I didn't warn you." She led him toward the tree near her fallen bag.

"My name's Mason, by the way."

But Emily didn't hear him. About sixteen inches up the base of the venerable aspen was what she'd traveled all this way to find.

****

"What *is* that?" Mason asked.

On her knees, Emily leaned even closer. Carved deeply into the wood was the unmistakable image of a human figure. "Hello, beautiful…"

The head was almost perfectly circular, as if it had been bored into the trunk with a round-tipped tool. The arms and legs were wedge-cut, each of a precise length so that the stick-figure retained realistic proportions. The grooves had been dug with such diligence that the tree had accepted them as part of its body, scarring them over and thus preserving them for Emily to find here today, lifetimes after they were rendered.

"Uh, ma'am?"

"The name's Emily," she said without taking her eyes from the carving. She dug a thin latex glove from her bag, pulled it on, and then delicately put her fingertip into the cuts.

"Okay. Emily. What are we looking at?"

"Time."

"I...don't understand."

"Time. That's what this is. A hundred years of it, if I'm right. Technically it's called a dendroglyph."

Once the word was out there—*dendroglyph*—it seemed to hang on the air with its own wings, as if it had further business and wasn't ready to drift away.

"I never heard of that before," Mason admitted.

"There are other names for it, like arborglyphs or tree carvings. Most aspens don't live beyond ninety years or so, but with sufficient water and the right conditions, like these have, they can hold out for a hundred and fifty years. I read that a hiker had spotted one out here, and sure enough..."

She traced the image with her finger, trying to imagine the face of the person who'd inscribed this image in this very tree so long ago. What was their name? Why had they come to this particular spot?

"So who put it here?"

Emily spared him a quick glance. Had he just read her thoughts? "A Spanish settler."

"You can tell by looking at it?"

She smiled. "That's my initial guess. There've been documented instances of dendroglyphs in a few places of the Pacific Northwest, and they're mostly linked to Basque or Irish immigrants. My hypothesis is that this one was made by a Spaniard."

"This isn't exactly the Pacific Northwest."

"And I'm not exactly doing sensible research. Or so I've been told." She returned to her inspection of the image, retrieving her phone from her satchel and taking a series of up-close shots.

"So...basically you're here to investigate antique

graffiti?"

"That's pretty much the reception I received when I made the proposal."

Hands raised, he backed up a step. "I didn't mean that like it sounded. Generally speaking, I'm not a smart ass."

"I'll have to take your word for it."

As good-looking as he might have been, Emily could spare him no time here at the epicenter of her search. She'd waited so long to find this; she might have been the first human being to see it since it had been inscribed on some afternoon before her grandmother was born.

"Can I ask one more question before leaving you in peace?"

"Go ahead."

"What's the significance of this?" He gestured at the carving. "Someone in the past, this Spanish guy of yours, whittled a picture in a tree. How does that…I don't know, do anything for your research?"

"That depends."

"On what?"

She finally took her eyes from the aspen, but only to let them roam the bases of the trees nearby. "On whether or not I can find any more before you cut them all down."

Chapter Six

Mason Hitapwa knew a meteorite when he saw one.

They didn't fall to earth very often. He went through his days seeing the same faces, staring up at the same sky. But now that sky had cracked, and this woman had hurtled through and reminded him of the night he'd stayed up to watch flaming rocks crackling like Roman candles between the stars.

"Would you like me to help you look?" He made the offer without considering it. Yes, he needed to get down to Rockerton and procure some lunch for the crew. Yes, he needed to face up to the concave shape now adorning the back of his foreman's truck. And yes to several other sensible things he should be doing. But there it was. "I mean, I know I'm supposed to be the guy who's chopping them down, but…"

Emily had already moved to the next aspen, circling it, fingers playing the bark in search of its special Braille. "Sorry. I didn't mean that to sound as bitter as it probably did. And I'm sure you have less monotonous things you could be doing."

"Are you kidding? You're the most fascinating person I've met in, oh, three or four hours, at least."

She stopped and looked around the tree at him, eyebrows midway up her brow. "That long, huh?"

"It's been a slow day."

27

"And your truck?"

"It's not going anywhere."

She seemed about to shake her head, but she was clearly too caught up in the thrill of her weird discovery to care one way or the other. "I suppose I shouldn't turn down another set of eyes. If you'd like to work in this direction, we can make sure we don't overlap or miss any trees. And you might need to look closely, because as the trees age, they begin to erase the dendroglyphs, like a wound healing."

Mason was happy for the diversion. If he admitted the truth to himself—which, as a rule, he tried to avoid—then he was a mid-thirties career logger who was fifty-two credit hours shy of a college degree and given to spending his evenings alone with a book and a bottle of wine he pretended was expensive. Tree-hopping in search of ancient scribbles sounded a lot better than going for lunch and resuming that particular routine.

"I'll start over here," he said.

"That's fine."

He chose a spot about fifteen feet away from her, squatted, and checked out the aspen in front of him. What was he looking for? He'd been seeing these trees for years now, with their pale bark striped with slashes of black. Aspens possessed what were called quaking leaves. That is, the rounded leaves would bend and quiver, either to protect them from strong winds or aid in photosynthesis—no one was really sure. He decided to make conversation by imparting this bit of woodland lore to Emily.

"*Populus tremuloides*," she said in return. "The leaves flutter in the breeze due to the flattened shape of their petioles."

"Uh, right. That, too."

"Did that sound as pretentious as I think?"

"It was a few rungs up the ladder, yeah."

"Sorry. Hazard of the trade. That's the one thing I swore not to inherit from my mentor."

"You work at a university?"

"For far too many years now, yes."

Mason was more than happy to continue this small talk as he crept through the trees, because when you discovered a meteorite in your backyard, you had only so long before the government showed up and trucked it away to a lab somewhere. He feared the same would soon happen with Emily. People who threw out Latin terms weren't the type to linger in these parts.

Something caught his eye.

He moved swiftly in that direction, his Hopi heritage never more evident than when he was alone in the wild. Making almost no sound, he sank to his knees near one of the thickest trunks in the area. There, about twenty inches up...

"Uh, ma'am?"

"It's Emily."

"Right. I think I may have found one of your symbols."

The words were hardly out of his mouth before she was bounding noisily through the underbrush and dropping down beside him. "Where?"

He pointed to what again appeared to be a crude human figure, although this time is was accompanied by a grouping of other, less-recognizable forms.

"Can you tell what those things are?" he asked.

"Maybe." From her bag she produced a clean and

decidedly not dog-eared notebook. Mason owned a similar journal-sized book, though his looked as if it might have gone cross-ways with a chainsaw, then spent a little time fermenting in a hollow log.

Emily flipped through the pages, whispering to herself.

Mason leaned closer to the tree, trying to make out the details. "When did you say these were carved?"

"I won't know for sure until I date them, and even then it's only a guess."

"You mean radiocarbon stuff?"

"Not exactly the same process, but it does involve lab work. One other way to nail down a time frame is by determining who these people were and when they were up here. I'll use exterior sources for that."

"Like early newspapers?"

"And court records, yes." She went from her notebook to the tree and back again.

"Well?"

She looked up at him. "He was a shepherd."

Mason, intrigued, studied the images. "So these four globs beside him…"

"Sheep."

"You're sure?"

"There was a time when this area was nothing but sheep-herders and cattlemen. They grazed these hills long before there were towns. In fact, the Rockerton civil archives contain several references to a full-fledged wool industry, at least on a small scale. There were at least four well-to-do ranch families based here, all of whom kept sheep."

As she spoke, her passion for it all was evident in her face. Some of her hair had escaped her ponytail and hung in front of her eyes. "Add to that the unknown number of small farms scattered around the mountain, and the odds of these being sheep are fairly strong."

Mason kept a straight face when he said, "Maybe they're pigs."

"Pigs?"

"Why not? My grandfather Jimmy White Cloud used to say that this land was built on bacon and ten-penny nails."

"I don't think anyone takes pigs up the mountain to graze."

"You sure?"

"Very."

Mason shrugged. "Just saying."

She went back to the carvings, and Mason smiled when she wasn't looking. It was nice to have met someone so enthused by their work that they were immune to sarcasm. He wondered if he'd been trying to use that sarcasm to flirt. It had been so long since he'd flirted, he couldn't be sure.

The sound of a ringing phone arrowed through the trees.

"That yours?" Emily asked.

Mason looked toward the truck, though he could no longer see it through the foliage. "Company phone. I left it in the cab."

"You get signal out here?"

"Satellites." He pointed skyward. "Straight from an angry boss to near-earth orbit and then down to a freshly dented truck."

"I'm really sorry about that. Seriously. I should've been paying more attention."

"The only attention you need to be paying is to

your shepherd there. And his pigs."

"Sheep."

"If you say so." Grinning, Mason jogged to the truck.

He looked back, hoping to see her watching him, but the trees had already concealed her.

****

Lightning bugs appeared, bearing fairy lanterns in the woods. Emily had been working for hours, and now that dusk was fully upon her, she realized two things: one, she'd managed to locate a total of four trees bearing dendroglyphs, and two, she was—without a doubt—lost.

"Hardly." Her voice sounded small and undignified out here. The crickets and other nameless night-bugs didn't pause in their symphony even to acknowledge her. She activated the GPS unit she wore around her neck. She'd taken care to log the position of each of her four blessed trees so as to be able to locate them again in the morning. The location of her humble campsite appeared as a black circle on the unit's tiny screen.

"West, then," she said to the gathering darkness. "Go west, young lady."

She struck off through the trees, wondering why she'd suddenly taken to talking to herself. Was the thrill of discovery making her giddy? The images she'd found on the third and fourth aspen had been no more revealing than the first two, being little more than faded renditions of the same human figure, both with and without his flock. Emily had photographed them extensively and made charcoal rubbings that were now carefully folded away in plastic bags.

So what? Magnelli asked her, challenging her,

prodding her to defend whatever the hell she was doing out here. *Doesn't sound like much to me.*

"Stuff it, sir." Exhaustion had knitted itself around her bones, and she didn't have the patience to argue, especially not with herself.

Thanks to the electronic marvel on its shoestring lanyard, she reached her basecamp and found it unmolested by raccoons. The lightning bugs were more prevalent here, mimicking the stars that were becoming visible through the treetops. Emily ate a meal of fruit and granola and tried not to think about the fact that she was alone in the woods, Gretel without a Hansel to hold her hand. She'd never been afraid of the dark, and every summer during her undergrad years she'd gone camping in Maine with sorority sisters and their beaus. So she knew her way around tent stakes and biodegradable shampoo. But still, the vastness of it all made her just a little bit afraid.

Then there came this unpleasant business of bathrooming in the wild. You didn't have your flat iron, you didn't have your ionic hair dryer with its fancy diffuser, and you damn sure didn't have a toilet. Emily had come armed with eco-friendly tissue, but putting it to use was not the most enjoyable of outdoors activities. She got it over with and decided that if her dissertation on the dendroglyphs didn't work out, she could always write a paper on the proper ways to squat in the weeds while avoiding poison sumac.

She stretched out on her sleeping bag but didn't zip the tent shut. Not yet. As she tucked her jacket under her head for a pillow, Mason's words returned to her.

You're the most fascinating person I've met in the last, oh, three or four hours, at least.

He was being facetious, of course. She'd never been called fascinating. *Eccentric*, certainly. Even *awkward* once or twice. Almost getting run over by a handsome stranger hadn't been on her agenda, but the encounter gave a mystical quality to a day so full of discovery that Emily doubted her ability to sleep. If only he didn't happen to represent the very people who were endangering her trees…

"Just my luck," she whispered. She lay there with the tent flap open, while outside the lightning bugs flickered with a Morse code she couldn't quite yet understand.

Chapter Seven

The next morning, her fieldbook open on the grass in front of her, Emily found the fifth message left by her long-dead shepherd.

This one was different. Generally, the carving was the same dimension, about six inches by three inches and so overgrown with bark as to be almost invisible, but the artist who'd put it here had added one characteristic not seen on the previous figure.

Hair.

Emily was certain of it. The fine strands around the head were not put there by wind nor accidentally scratched there by a passing animal. They were carved just as deeply as the figure itself and looked equally as old. She scooted closer, aware that her pulse had picked up a bit. She sensed this was about more than a shepherd simply cutting his mark into a tree to pass the time while his flock grazed. This was telling a story.

"So what do you say to that?" she asked no one in particular. Maybe she was talking to Magnelli or maybe to God. It didn't matter. Neither answered.

The growl of an approaching vehicle was followed by two quick bursts of its horn.

Emily looked up, frozen. Only occasionally did she hear the sound of the men working along the hillside, so to have a noise so loud and so near—

Another honk.

"Mason?"

She got to her feet, made a futile effort to wipe the dampness from her knees, and then wove through the labyrinth until she saw him.

He wore the same bedraggled denim jacket, but his shirt today was vibrant white and open at the throat, revealing a triangle of dusky skin. Emily decided that he looked exactly like what he was, an outdoorsman. One who wasn't adorned with the trappings that she associated with the type: no camouflage, no knife sheath on his belt, no ring-shaped bulge of snuff can in his pocket.

As he approached, he said, "I was in the neighborhood."

"Is that a fact?"

"Heard there was a crazy scientist from back East tromping around in the woods."

"I try and make it a point never to *tromp*."

"Well, maybe it's not you, then. Woman I'm looking for is said to be hot on the trail of some runaway pigs from the past."

Emily fought her smile. "Sorry, haven't seen her."

He stopped a few feet away from her, then glanced toward the spot where she'd made her findings. "I looked up the word *symbologist*."

"And?"

"You're interested in how different cultures express themselves through the literal marks they make on the world."

"More or less."

"You're a type of anthropologist?"

"That's the general umbrella field for this, yes."

Mason indicated the truck. It wasn't the same one

he'd driven yesterday. "Borrowed a new ride."

"So…what happened with…"

"My boss and the fender bender?"

She nodded.

"He's been madder."

"I'm sorry. I really am."

"No big deal. I told him I was taking the day off, and he thought that was probably a good idea because he was already sick of looking at me." Mason pointed toward the trees. "I was thinking that…maybe you'd like some help. Finding the symbols, I mean."

In another life, perhaps Emily had been more ready with a glib response when rough-around-the-edges men appeared in the middle of the forest and offered to assist her. She wished for more of that person's moxie as she stood there rather flatfooted and groped for a reply.

"Forget it," he said, suddenly unable to look at her. "Technically, I'm the enemy. You don't want a log-cutter mucking around with your trees."

"No, wait. It's okay. That sounds…beneficial."

Beneficial? She groaned inside. Could she possibly come off sounding more like a geeky academic? "Thanks for the offer. I won't turn down an extra pair of eyes. I, uh, just found another one, by the way."

"More pigs?"

She shook her head.

"Goats?"

She allowed herself a fleeting grin. "If you're going to poke fun—"

"No more." He held up both hands. "I promise."

"Good. Come on, then. I might as well introduce you to the woman I just met."

He hurried to catch up with her. "Woman?"

"She has long hair. She's definitely a *her*."

"The shepherd's a girl?"

"No, but he knows one."

"Ah, the plot thickens."

"And then some."

They walked into the trees.

****

"...but I finally wore them down and convinced them it was a worthy project," Emily said as she worked, moving in a crouch from one tree to the next. "Of course, I'm out here on my own dime, which means my coach may turn into a pumpkin and I'll have to limp home in defeat if I don't come up with something in the next few weeks." She stopped what she was doing and peered at him from around a trunk. "Am I rambling?"

"On the proverbial scale from one to ten?"

"Sure."

"Seven."

"That's it? Seven's not so bad."

"Maybe seven-point-five."

"Sorry. I usually do this kind of thing alone. I'm not used to having an audience."

"Hey, I'm learning a lot. You're talking to someone who's never been east of the Mississippi, so consider me undaunted by your seven-point-five."

"Let's just call it a seven."

"Deal."

Emily returned to the aspen in front of her. What she'd said was true: she *wasn't* a talker by nature. Normally she was intent on observation, a watcher of people and quiet recorder of life. She supposed it was the anthropology streak in her, the desire to soak up the nuances of those around her and make sense of them. People fascinated her. All of this made her an award-winning listener—her friends were said as much—but she'd also been accused of being the I-word.

"Actually I'm an introvert," she admitted.

"Nothing wrong with that."

"Tell that to my mother. She spent her life trying to transform her wall flower daughter into a socialite."

"I can relate. My grandfather wanted me to study medicine. But I just don't have the heart for it."

"I think all grandparents would probably want their grandchildren to be doctors."

"Not that kind of medicine. He was a seer."

"Oh." Emily had no idea what to say to that. She kept on working.

"My grandfather foretold the weather and expelled spirits. He made the corn grow. Me, I'm lucky if I can keep my geranium alive. It's gasping its last green breath in my bedroom window as we speak."

In her studies, Emily had read about Native cultures, but not extensively. Her specialty was the European immigrants of the early twentieth century and the ways they transplanted their culture to the Americas. The realist in her doubted the existence of spirits, but the little girl who still lived inside of her liked the idea of believing in them.

"I guess I'm not a very good Indian," Mason said.

Emily thought she saw something, so she leaned close, her face mere inches from the tree. "In my line of work, we tend to favor the term *Native American*."

"Yeah, a white man invented that phrase. Never met an Indian who used it. We might say *native people* when referring to the aboriginals as a whole, but mostly we're just Indians. Well, *half* Indian for some of us."

Emily decided this one wasn't a symbol of any kind, but just a random scratch. Her wishful thinking was causing her to see patterns that didn't exist.

"Can I ask you a question?"

Emily tapped the tree as if chastising it for its inability to provide her with a treasure. "Sure, go ahead."

"This shepherd…is there any chance he would've done more than just carve pictures into the trees?"

"I'm not sure what you mean."

"Like, say he drilled a hole in the tree and stuffed something inside."

Emily, intrigued, leaned around the aspen. She couldn't quite see Mason; only a single battered boot was visible through the foliage. "What have you found?"

"I don't know for sure. But I think you better come have a look."

Chapter Eight

Emily dropped down next to Mason and homed in on where he was pointing. The two of them bent closer, side by side, as rapt as children staring through a window at winter's first snow.

"What is it?" she asked.

"You tell me."

The dendroglyph was by now unmistakable, as simple as a cave drawing but clearly human in form. Near the figure's hand was a deeply indented circle, the edges of which were layered in a black ring of natural scarring.

"Looks like a bullet hole," Mason said.

"There's something in there." She put her finger in the hole and tapped the obstruction with a fingernail that was in semi-desperate need of an emery board. "That sounds like...metal."

"Seriously? Let me see."

Before Emily could say anything, Mason flattened himself on his stomach and wiggled as close to the tree as he could get, trying to peer into the hole. The shadows thwarted him. "I can't tell one way or the other."

"Touch it."

Mason performed the same tap test. "I'll be damned."

Her breath quickening, Emily opened the bag that

was slung over her shoulder and explored its contents until she found the little flashlight she'd brought along. Abandoning all regard for decorum, she lay down in the grass.

"Why would there be anything metal in there?" Mason wondered.

Emily became aware of him beside her, their shoulders pressed together as they observed the anomaly in the bark. On any other day she would've withdrawn a little—after all, she'd known this man for only twenty-four hours. But suddenly her personal space seemed less important than the act of shared discovery.

The metal was set almost two inches deep in the tree. "It looks like a plug of some kind," she said.

"Or a belly button."

"Yes, or that."

"The shepherd put it here?"

"I honestly don't know." She held the light steady. "I suppose that the tree would have continue to grow around the object."

"So what is it?"

"Do you want my most professional response?"

"Sure."

"Then I have absolutely no idea, professional or otherwise."

Mason laughed. "That makes two of us." He turned to look at her, his face only inches from hers. "Hey."

She met his eyes. "Yes?"

"Do you want me to dig it out?"

"I don't know. It seems to be wedged fairly deep."

"I have tools in the truck."

Emily saw the delight in his eyes, the boyhood

enthusiasm for this mystery they'd found.

"Well?" he asked.

She set him to the task with a nod, unaware of how that simple gesture would put in motion everything that was to come.

****

"I don't want to damage the tree," Emily said as Mason set to work with a hammer and chisel. "It's probably been standing here since Teddy Roosevelt was president."

"I may be a logger," Mason told her, lying on his side and working like a mechanic under a car, "but that doesn't mean I always resort to an axe. He was a conservationist, by the way."

"Who?"

"Roosevelt. He created a lot of national parks."

"How do you know that?"

"I read a lot, at least when I'm not busy mowing down forests." He grinned up at her to let her know he was teasing.

Teasing? she wondered. *Have we advanced to the teasing stage?* She shoved the thought aside. She wouldn't permit herself to be distracted when she was so close to…what? She wasn't sure what she was about to find, but she was certain that the shepherd had left her a gift.

"He would've liked this place," Mason said.

"We're still talking about Roosevelt?"

Mason tapped the chisel around the edges of the metal plug. "You have something against discussing your presidents?"

"That particular field of American history isn't exactly my specialty."

43

"Remind me to tell you about the *Hopituh Shi-nu-mu*."

Emily wasn't familiar with the term, though she appreciated its exotic sound. She was far more concerned with whatever Mason was digging from the aspen's trunk. "How's it coming?"

"Slowly. This thing is really wedged in here. The tree's completely encased it."

She watched him work. Mason had removed his jacket and hung it from a branch. He handled the tools with agility, flicking pieces of wood from around the edge of the metal. Emily felt like pacing out of excitement but managed to keep still. What was taking him so long?

"What happened to these shepherds, anyway?" Mason asked.

"Time, I guess."

"What do you mean.?"

"It's the same thing that happened to rotary telephones. People found a more efficient way of doing things and moved on. Shepherds are a rare breed these days."

"Telephones, huh?"

"What I mean is that professions change just like technology changes. You don't have shepherds anymore, or cobblers or blacksmiths or men who repair covered wagons."

He tightened his jaw and inserted the chisel a bit deeper. "This is one of those times that I'm reminded how I was born too late. I would've made a first-rate covered-wagon repairman."

"Careful," Emily warned. "Don't hurt yourself on my account."

"Can't hold back now. In for a penny, and all of that…" He cleared a sufficient gap in the wood, then used the chisel as a lever and forced the plug to slide forward.

Emily bit her bottom lip between her teeth.

When half an inch of the metal was protruding from the hole, Mason switched to a pair of pliers and clamped down on it. Bracing himself against the tree, he pulled, biceps swelling his shirt sleeve. "Sure is…tight."

Swept away in anticipation, Emily joined him in the task, boldly putting her hands around his. She forced her heels into the soft ground for leverage.

The two of them, both holding the pliers, pulled as one and the shepherd's gift, hammered into the tree decades before Emily was born, slipped free of its moorings.

"We got it!" Mason shouted.

Emily examined it as he held it up, still gripped in the pliers' jaws. It was a metal cylinder about three inches long and half an inch in diameter, rusted so completely that it was the color of something found on Mars.

"What is it?" he asked, his excitement evident in his voice.

"Is there a cap on the end?" She took the tube from the pliers and let it rest in her palm. It looked like nothing, really. Just a piece of oxidized junk. "Is there anything else in the hole?"

Mason took her flashlight and studied the hollow space he'd made. "That's a negative."

Emily held the artifact to her ear and shook it.

"Anything?"

"Maybe." She did it again. Was there something inside of it? Or was that just her usual wishful-thinking self playing tricks on her?

"Any way to open it?" he asked.

"Only if we cut it. Is that possible?"

"Not without a hacksaw. You didn't happen to bring one along, did you?"

There he was, teasing her again. "Sorry. I left it on the kitchen table next to my cutting torch."

"Sounds like an interesting kitchen."

"That's how we roll in New Jersey." She got to her feet. "I need to see inside of this thing."

He hopped up. "I have a couple of handsaws in the truck, but they're made for wood, not steel or iron or whatever that thing's made of. But I have the right kind of blade in my garage." He held up a hand. "Now, I'm not asking you over to my place or anything. It's not like that. We can drive into Rockerton and pick up a hacksaw at the hardware store. I'm letting you know that the option is available. *Mi* garage, *su* garage."

Emily considered it. She didn't know this man. But already she trusted him, which made no sense at all. Maybe it was the way he transformed into a boy when hunting for buried treasure in the woods and then into a man when he looked at her. Or maybe she was just so curious to crack open the cylinder that her better judgment got tossed out like a pair of open-toed pumps two seasons out of fashion. "Promise me you're not a serial killer," she said.

"Only if you promise me the same thing. You could be Lizzy Borden, for all I know."

"Would you like to search my purse for an axe?"

He glanced at her soiled handbag. "You couldn't fit

46

an axe in there, but certainly a really sharp hatchet."

She rolled her eyes. "Come on, native guide. Lead the way."

Chapter Nine

The cabin stood on a shelf of land that overlooked the valley and the town below. It reminded Emily of the pictures she'd seen of Abe Lincoln's boyhood home, a modest log construction with a single chimney and few windows. Unlike Abe's, this one sported a wraparound porch, single-car garage, and a weathervane in the shape of Elvis.

"It's nice," she said as she climbed out of the truck. "Looks cozy."

"Keeps the rain off my head. I guess people on the East Coast don't do a lot of building with pine logs."

"Or any other kind of logs, for that matter. Did you build it yourself?"

"Bought it off a former prospector who was about a hundred and eighty years old when he passed on. Alzheimer's never got him. He was sharp right up to the end. He gave me my first job when I moved up here from Arizona ten years ago. Said he built it to withstand everything from snowstorms to angry wives."

The grass was neatly trimmed, the wood of the porch rail polished so that it gleamed. Emily wondered if he kept the interior in a similar pristine yet rustic condition. Maybe for once in her adult life she'd gotten lucky. The last four single men she'd met had been so unremarkable that she probably wouldn't be able to pick them out in a police lineup.

Mason welcomed her into the garage, which was apparently not intended for vehicles whatsoever. The products of the woodworker's trade took up every available space. Around the perimeter was a variety of tools, table saws, and workbenches. In the center of the floor was a handmade bassinet of exquisite detail. The wood of this infant's bed was finely tooled with delicate scrollwork, and the legs were carved to resemble children's building blocks.

Emily didn't know what to say. "Did you..." She could only gesture toward it.

He shrugged while searching for the hacksaw. "That's what happens when a guy doesn't have cable TV. Idle hands, you know."

Emily approached the bassinet and ran her hand along the rich wood. It was as fine as any piece of furniture she'd seen for sale in the priciest New York shops—not that she had much experience with expensive home decor, but she knew quality when she was standing in front of it. "This is...it's beautiful."

"And time consuming. If I'd known it was going to take so long, I would've charged them a bit more."

"You sell furniture?"

"Cabinets, mostly. But sometimes I get an off-the-wall request, and I'm just obsessive-compulsive enough to lose sleep over it until it's done. Ah, here we go." He located the proper saw and then clamped the metal tube into a desk-mounted vise.

"I suppose this isn't proper form," Emily said as she took up a position at the end of the desk. "There are correct ways to handle archaeological finds, and then there's this."

"Would you rather ship it off to a lab somewhere

and let them have the pleasure of opening it?"

"Not on your life."

"Thought so." He set the saw's teeth against the metal and gave it a few tentative strokes. Rust flaked off like chipped paint.

"Keep it as close to the end as possible," Emily advised. "I want to minimize the risk of damaging whatever's in there."

"Could be empty. Maybe it's just dirt you heard rattling inside."

"He wouldn't have inserted it into the tree if it was empty."

Mason worked the saw carefully back and forth, taking his time. "Maybe not. Or maybe he was just bored that afternoon. Watching the flock can't be a very stimulating pastime."

"I suppose we'll see."

Thirty seconds later, a dime-sized circle of metal fell away, hit the floor, and rolled until becoming mired in a pile of sawdust. Mason loosened the vise, then gave the open tube to Emily.

She accepted it like she was handling nitroglycerin. She imagined she could smell the century-old air escaping this little time capsule in her hand. Peering inside, she saw nothing but darkness. She turned it upside down.

A slender coil of paper dropped onto her palm.

Emily held her breath at the sight. The paper was brown and cracked and tight, like a hand-rolled cigarette. How long had it resided in its cocoon, waiting to be found? And why was she so privileged as to receive it?

Mason passed a hand through his hair. "Wow."

"Yeah."

"Are you, uh, going to unroll it?"

"I think I'm afraid to."

"It could crumble to pieces."

"Sure could." She dared to touch it with a fingernail. It felt solid enough. Perhaps its airtight casing had preserved it. "Do you have tweezers?"

"In the house."

"Would you mind?"

"The bathroom's just inside the back door. Follow me. Just ignore the underwear I've got strewn all over the floor."

Emily assumed he was kidding, but she was too intent on her prize to pay much attention. This was more than she'd expected. Locating simplistic drawings on tree trunks was one thing, but finding a message in an aspen bottle was entirely another.

"Watch your step."

When she looked around, she was standing in a short hallway with a utility room on her left and a guest restroom on her right. In front of her was what looked to be a living room. From what she could see of it, the hardwood floor was immaculate and the furniture made by the same gifted hand that had created the bassinet behind her.

Mason flipped on the bathroom light and found the tweezers in a first-aid kit he kept beneath the sink. "Let's use the kitchen table. Ignore the dogs playing poker. It was the only art I could afford."

Emily was not surprised to see that he was joking again. There were no card-playing poodles. Instead, there were half a dozen tall bookcases, each filled beyond capacity. The kitchen was well-stocked and spotless. A lush rug of multi-colored threads covered most of the living-room floor. The painting above the mantel was of a young Indian boy reaching for the sun.

They went to work at a thick rosewood table that Emily suspected he'd made himself. As she settled into one of the matching chairs, she noticed a single photo fixed to the side of the refrigerator, almost forgotten in the shadows. Pictured there was a beautiful woman with black hair nearly down to her waist. She wore a turquoise necklace and stared into the distance as if searching the horizon.

"So let's see what we have," Mason said, taking a seat across from her.

Had he seen her studying the woman's picture? Emily wasn't sure. She redirected her attention to the paper, placing it on the table and then using the tweezers and one finger to gently unroll it.

"I take it back," he said.

"Take what back?"

"Yesterday I said you were the most fascinating person I'd met in three or four hours. This definitely makes me reconsider."

"I hope I don't disappoint you."

"No chance of that."

The shepherd's words appeared one at a time, rendered so faintly that they were almost invisible. When the paper slip was entirely unfurled, it was six inches long, containing three lines of script written in an uncertain hand.

Mason got up and swung around to her side of the table in order to read over her shoulder. "Uh, what language is this?"

"Castilian, I suspect."

"Castilian?"

"The type of Spanish primarily spoken in Spain."

"Oh. I don't suppose you savvy *español*."

"Only a little. I minored in French as an undergrad. How about you?"

"I have some First Mesa."

"Some what?"

"A Hopi dialect. In other words, I'm no help."

Emily let her eyes roam the foreign words. Spanish was one of the Romance languages, a descendent of Latin and familiar enough to her that she could manage an effective pronunciation if not a definition. "There *is* one word here that I know, however."

"Yeah? What is it?"

"*Amor.*"

"Meaning?"

She looked up from the paper. "Love."

****

Mason handed her a bottle of water from his fridge and opened one of his own. She watched him drink slowly. She was glad that she hadn't made this discovery on her own. Sharing it somehow made it real.

"So how do we decipher it?" he asked. "I have a friend, Luiz, who speaks Spanish. I'm sure he wouldn't mind giving us a translation."

"The researcher in me appreciates the old-school approach, but we can probably do it a lot faster." She held up her phone.

"Ah. Right. Can you tell I don't spend much time online?"

"I don't blame you. You're not missing much. But I'm not getting very good signal. Can I use your WiFi?"

"Would you settle for a computer plugged in the

old-fashioned way?"

"You're not still on dial-up, are you?"

He laughed. "It's not quite that bad. Come on." He led her to a small office adjacent to the garage. The lyrics of John Lennon's "Imagine" hung above the computer's antiquated monitor. "They don't make 'em like they used to," he said.

"They certainly don't."

Mason initiated a lengthy boot-up process, reminding Emily how accustomed she'd grown to instant access to information. Usually a few fingertips on a touch-screen connected her with the digital world; strange, that so much wisdom—from Archimedes to Oprah—awaited her online, while the only knowledge she cared about had been locked away in a primitive forest for over a hundred years.

"Sometimes I get in a really good nap while I'm waiting," he said.

"It's not so bad." In truth, though, she was so anxious to translate the note that she wanted to shout at this prehistoric computer to please, if you don't mind, get your silicon ass in gear. It was then that she noticed another snapshot of the woman with the black hair. This one was small and stuck to a filing cabinet with a magnet. She was of Native descent, with a faultless complexion and sad, earth-colored eyes.

"Houston, we have contact." Mason poked at the keyboard with two fingers and entered his password, and a few seconds later, his homepage appeared: the Colorado Online Readers Club. He looked at her with an embarrassed grin. "I'm sort of a book nerd at heart. That's a state secret, so don't tell the guys."

"I'll take it to my grave."

"Thanks. So where are we going?"

"Any translation site is fine."

"Uh, maybe you should take over," he suggested. "I have a hunch that your typing skills are slightly more advanced than mine."

"You won't get any better without practice."

"I'll save the practice for the next ancient manuscript we uncover. This one's all yours."

Emily took his seat when he got up. As she typed, she wondered who the woman in the picture was and why she even cared. "Okay, we're here. Can you unroll it again?"

Mason took his turn with the tweezers, exposing the faint script. Emily had heard of scholars making discoveries—Aztec tablets, scrolls in clay jars, and lost Elizabethan plays hidden away in London attics—but she'd never made one herself. Until now.

Mason read the words and spelled them as necessary, though Emily was smart enough not to trust her shepherd's spelling prowess. She'd need to make educated guesses about his intentions and hope the translator wasn't too picky.

"That's it," he said, carefully returning the slip of paper to its former state. "What do we have?"

Satisfied that she'd accurately input the text, Emily clicked TRANSLATE.

A new page slowly loaded.

"Behold the wonder that is my modem," Mason said.

"Could be worse."

"We could fly to Spain and back before this thing gets anywhere."

"It's fine."

Mason opened his mouth to reply, but then the text appeared on the screen, and they both leaned forward intently. Emily read it aloud, automatically correcting the foibles of the translator so that the sentences sounded as their author had intended. "'She meets me today at our special place. I will write more later and tell the trees of my Sarita, my love.'"

She read it again, silently this time.

Mason left the computer, paced, and turned around. "Emily?"

She didn't look away from the monitor. "Yes?"

"Is this for real?"

She turned to him. "This note has been hidden out there for a long time."

"*How* long?"

"I don't know."

"Who is this guy, this shepherd?"

"I don't know that, either."

Mason gathered a breath and put his hands on his hips. He exhaled. "I can't even begin to tell you how cool it is to be a part of this."

"You don't have to tell me. I already know."

She returned to the words and read them again, slower this time, lingering on the woman's name. "*Sarita...*"

Chapter Ten

The next morning, Mason drove to work with the radio off. This was abnormal. Usually he tuned to any station that would allow him to harmonize with the Bee Gees or the Eagles or any other band too old for him. The modern stuff failed to speak to him. But today he didn't have time for "Desperado." He couldn't stop thinking of the shepherd's story and the woman who'd introduced it to him.

"The woman and the trees," he said to himself as he navigated the narrow hillside track. The pickup bucked over the uneven ground, threatening to slosh his coffee. Mason drove with one hand, holding his cup in the other and trying not to spill it in his lap. Emily had left shortly after they'd translated the note, off to call her professor and dazzle him with her success.

"*Our* success," he amended. Hadn't he been the one to find the metal pipe in the tree? Certainly so. But could he legitimately claim any of the credit?

"Nope," he said, shaking his head with a smile. The best part of it all had been seeing Emily's face as everything came together. Her sense of wonder had only intensified her beauty. But of course, none of that mattered. What kind of future was there for a woman who read the aspens and a man who sawed them down?

"None at all." He needed to keep his head at a practical angle and remind himself that sometimes two people simply came from different worlds.

His coffee survived the trip. Chewing on his thoughts and not particularly liking the taste, Mason parked with the other company vehicles near the RV that served as the crew's mobile headquarters, then went in to see the foreman.

Larry Ellsworth looked up from his laptop. "You survive your day off?"

"More or less."

"You're one of them guys who have to be forced to take vacation time. Almost as annoying as the ones who try and take too much."

"Sorry, boss."

"Sit down."

Mason took a seat in front of the desk, on the corner of which was a small resin figurine of a comical golfer. On the statuette's base was Ellsworth's motto: THE UGLIER A MAN'S LEGS, THE BETTER HE PLAYS GOLF. Mason had seen it a thousand times, and now he looked right through it. He kept seeing Emily's face in the glow of the monitor as she read the shepherd's note.

"Talked to the insurance company," Ellsworth said.

Mason blinked, and Emily faded. "And?"

"Repairs on the dent are going to ding us for eight-hundred bucks. With a five-hundred-dollar deductible, looks like we're taking that out of your paycheck in two installments."

Mason absorbed this with remarkable detachment. Normally he would've cringed at the thought of losing such a substantial wedge of his salary pie graph. But now it didn't seem so important. He was much more interested in learning what else the shepherd was going to tell the trees. Had he hidden more messages out there?

"That okay with you?" Ellsworth asked.

"Uh, yeah, that seems fair."

"Just like that?"

"It was my fault. So, yeah. Just like that."

"Outstanding. Then on to the next project." Ellsworth touched a few keys on his laptop and then spun the computer around so that it faced Mason. On the screen was a topographical map of the surrounding fifty-mile area. "I want you to prep the crew on our next move. You're basically my second in command out here, despite your shitty driving skills, so it's time you carried a bit more of the load. You could stand for a raise, right?"

"I wouldn't turn it down."

"You're due for one in another couple of months, help you offset all that repair work. In the meantime, get us ready to work this area here." He tapped the screen. "Quadrant four-twelve."

Mason nodded. The company's contract strictly outlined which areas they could cut and how many loads they could remove from each quadrant. Moving all the men and machines to a new region was an all-day affair and could prove logistically cumbersome. Ellsworth usually handled those duties himself. The fact that he was entrusting them to Mason—

Wait a moment. Mason studied the coordinates on the screen. Wasn't Emily's camp set up just west of there?

"I'll print this off," Ellsworth said, spinning the laptop back around. "You can get started with the small gear immediately. Oh, and make sure you use one of the newer radios. Those old things tend to lose signal at the worst possible moment."

Mason moved his tongue worriedly behind his teeth.

"There a problem?"

He waved it away. "Just fazed out for a moment."

"Yeah, well don't be fazing the next time you're in a company truck. If they jack up our insurance premiums, I wouldn't be counting on you getting that raise."

"Understood." He got up and headed for the door, wondering if the shepherd's trees would encroach on the land recently tagged for clear-cutting.

"Hey, Mace."

He stopped and turned back around. "Yeah?"

"Are you forgetting something?" Ellsworth pointed at the line of walkie-talkies resting on their charging bases. "New radio."

"Oh, right. Sorry." He snagged one and clipped it to his belt.

"Something bothering you, man?"

"Do I look bothered?"

"A little."

He faked a smile. "Just another day in paradise." He left the RV, closed the door, and listened to the distant chorus of chainsaws.

For now, Emily's aspens were safe, as they stood just outside the quadrant. But the shepherd seemed to have chosen his trees at random, and there could very well be some undiscovered ones standing within the cutting zone. If there were some kind of pattern to the shepherd's choice of trees, then it would be easier to locate them. Was there such a design?

"I don't know," Mason said to no one but the wind. He wanted to alert Emily to the possible danger, but he didn't have her number. Besides, by now she'd be wading through the woods, her cell phone probably turned off for want of a decent signal. She was more concerned with dendroglyph enigmas than she was with taking calls from random loggers who wanted an excuse just to talk to her.

With no better options, Mason donned his hardhat and went about the business of getting his crew prepared to move to the last place on earth he wanted them.

****

Sarita.

With that name guiding her, Emily ran her hands along the bark, searching for the slightest imperfection. After getting a room at one of Rockerton's two motels, she'd spent yesterday evening carefully recording the information she'd gathered so far, including the exact coordinates of each tree the shepherd had marked and the dimensions of his carved figures. She emailed her findings to Magnelli, who was impressed enough to call her within minutes of receiving it.

That note is a piece of history, he'd told her. *You need to take steps to preserve it.*

She'd followed his instructions, but this was a new day and now thoughts of her mentor were not even vague shapes on her horizon. She thought only of Sarita.

Well, that was *almost* true.

An hour ago she'd realized that the possibility of discovery wasn't so fine when you had no one with whom to share it. Sarita may have been in her heart, but

Emily would've liked someone a bit more...tangible.

The aspen in front of her demanded her attention. Satisfied that this particular specimen concealed no secrets, she moved methodically to the next, determined to touch every tree in the Rocky Mountains if necessary.

She moved east.

Hours passed. She took several breaks, letting her eyes relax and the muscles in her lower back unwind. The forest had a way of blinding you. Because everything looked so much the same, you had a tendency to gloss over the details. She had to concentrate so as not to miss anything. A headache formed just behind her eyes, and she cursed herself for not bringing any aspirin to her campsite.

As she stood with her water bottle, watching a squirrel make a snack of some crumbs from her protein bar, she considered how fortunate she was. Recently thirty years old, slowly closing in on her doctoral degree, and currently in the midst of exciting research. Other than a few new wrinkles at the corners of her eyes and—omigod—that single gray hair which showed up a month ago and had promptly been plucked out, she had no complaints. Things hadn't always been on the upswing like this. Things hadn't always been so fair.

At seventeen she'd fallen in love with a college freshman whose claim to criminal fame was a drug habit he tried to conceal but couldn't. If he hadn't been such a charmer and so damn good looking, and had Emily not been so lacking in self-esteem, she wouldn't have followed him down that broken path. She never went so far as to use the hard stuff, but for two years she existed for no other purpose but to listen to neo-hippies play music on the Jersey shore.

She took a long drink, tried to forget it all, and failed.

Even after that first relationship ended, she only spiraled farther down, latching on to guitar players and guys with dreadlocks and anyone who made her feel wanted for more than a weekend. At the time, she'd called it living. But it wasn't. You couldn't really live until you did so with a sense of self-worth. Emily was twenty years old and about to flunk out of Atlantic Cape Community College before she found any reason to claim an identity, and now—a decade later—she wore it like armor. Most of the time, anyway.

She chided herself for giving in to the memories, and then she saw it—a rune on the tree.

She ran through the underbrush and dropped to her knees. This tree was wider than the others, many of its branches sporting no leaves. If the tree wasn't dead, it was well on its way. Carved into the trunk about two feet up was something she hadn't seen before.

The shepherd was here again, but beside him was a different shape, a circle with one flattened end. This symbol was larger than the shepherd himself. What did it represent? His house? A boulder? The moon?

Emily slung the bag from her shoulder and pulled out her phone, her notebook, and her sketchpad to produce a rubbing. She set to work making every possible recording, measuring the depth of the cuts and the exact spacing between the figures. She didn't know how much time passed, but at some point she became aware of a honking horn.

She looked up.

"Emily? You out here?"

"Mason." She jumped to her feet, eager to reveal her latest find. "*Over here!*"

She watched him jog through the trees. He was lean and quick, a man at ease in his own body. Emily's circle of friends was limited to the professionals she knew in academia. Most of those men, unfortunately, were either socially awkward or so infatuated by the Ph.D. hanging on their office wall that they'd never know the simple joy of running through the woods. The last one she'd dated, Dr. Norris Cook, had been gentlemanly and serene and entirely incapable of talking about anything but late nineteenth-century British writers. As profound as the novel *David Copperfield* might have been, it was no way to spice up a Saturday night.

He stopped a few feet in front of her. "Hey."

"Fancy meeting you here."

"Rumor has it that there's a lady druid out here casting spells on the trees. They sent me to make sure everything was okay."

"It's more than okay, actually."

"You found another one?"

For some reason, he didn't look as happy about that as Emily had expected. Was he already losing interest in her quest? "What's wrong?"

He shrugged it off. "Nothing. Just out of shape, I guess. Remind me not to go sprinting over hill and dale again. Let's see what you've got."

They knelt together at the tree.

"See this?" She touched the rounded shape next to the figure she was now thinking of as Sarita's lover, rather than simply the shepherd. Now he had a purpose greater than watching his flock. "I haven't been able to make any sense of it."

Mason followed the curves with his finger. "There's nothing around here that looks like this, is there?"

"Not that I can see."

"Is it a hill? Maybe a mound of earth somewhere along the mountain slope?"

"I've studied the map, but—"

"So it's a metaphor. You're the symbologist. If this isn't a literal interpretation of a geological feature, then what could it symbolize? I mean, to me this looks sort of like a man being swallowed by a cloud."

"When I was young, I used to walk along the beach at Cape May. The tide would make patterns in the sand. I'd stare at them for hours and imagine faces in the lines—animals, ships, all kinds of things. That's what this is like. It would be almost impossible to guess what Sarita's lover was trying to say if he's speaking figuratively."

"Maybe we'll get lucky."

"Our frame of reference is entirely different than his. We have no way of seeing through his eyes."

"Yeah? Is it really so different?" Mason sat back on the soft grass and wrapped his arms around his knees. "He sounds like a guy with a crush on a girl. That's a pretty universal frame of reference. It's been around since Adam first passed a note to Eve and asked her to check yes or no."

Emily couldn't help herself: she laughed.

"Seriously," Mason insisted. "I bet this dude was just like me."

"Dude?"

"That's what guys like the shepherd and me call

each other. He and I are tight. We go way back." He crossed his fingers and held them up to demonstrate this close brotherly connection.

Emily was happy to play along. "Is that so?"

"As a matter of fact, I know exactly what he was doing out here."

"Hopefully he was protecting his family's wool investment."

"Nah, that was just a cover story. You see"—He plucked a blade of grass and put it in his mouth like a proper knave—"there was this certain girl that lived at the next farm."

"Sarita."

"Right on. She had hair like, well, probably a lot like yours."

"Unbrushed and full of split ends?"

"And like you, she enjoyed playing in the woods."

"I haven't been *playing*, thank you very much."

Mason ignored her. "Now this shepherd had a problem, though. His father fully intended for him to marry someone else, the daughter of the Rockerton mayor." He frowned. "Rockerton was around back then, wasn't it?"

"It wasn't incorporated as a city, but there were about a hundred residents at the turn of the century." Her research had told her that there were actually a hundred and eleven, but she wasn't about to get hung up on the details. Not now.

"So maybe they had a mayor," Mason said.

"Possibly."

"And he had a daughter."

"Possibly."

"And *she* was thin as a rail spike, with mean eyes

and a nasty disposition."

Emily wondered what had turned him into a sudden storyteller but wasn't about to interrupt his momentum by asking. "She wasn't the one the shepherd wanted to marry."

"Oh, he might have listened to his father, under other circumstances. He didn't really have a lot to choose from in a town of a hundred people. But as fate would have it, there was Sarita."

Emily had already decided she adored the name. The Spanish sound of it was just evident enough to intrigue her. "And then what happened?"

Mason looked as if he were about to deliver the climax of his story, but then his face changed. There was a sadness there he couldn't conceal.

"What?" Emily pressed. "What's the matter?"

He took the strand of grass from his mouth and stared at it.

"Mason, please."

He looked up. "I'm going to cut down the shepherd's trees. All of them."

Chapter Eleven

They walked through the forest together, eyes on the ground.

Typical, Emily thought. *The hunk with the shy smile and good sense of humor works for the dark side.* She shouldn't have been surprised. It was par for the course of her relationships.

"Not talking to me won't help anything,"

"What is there to say? I work for a logging company. We hold a contract with the state to work certain sections of the county. This is one of those sections."

"Right here? Right on top of us?"

"Almost. The quadrant starts about a quarter mile east of your camp."

"But one of the dendroglyphs we found is…that's precisely where it is."

He put his hands in his pockets. "I know."

"And there could be more of them. A lot more."

"I know that, too."

Emily bit back the next word that came to her. It would have served no purpose other than to make Mason feel even worse than he already did. Still, she wasn't about to let him think he could do this to her and come out clean. "Do you have any idea how old some of these trees are? Do you?" She kept going before he had a chance to respond. "The oldest have been standing for a hundred and fifty years. *A hundred and fifty*. And you know what's even worse? A few of them are the last links we have to the people who used to live here. Those dendroglyphs out there aren't just random sketches somebody made to pass the time. They're a man's attempt to tell a story, to say something about himself and why he bothered getting up in the morning. And no, I'm not reading more into it than is actually there. You saw his note. You know what mattered to him."

Mason spoke so softly that she almost didn't hear him: "I don't know what you want me to say."

"Say this makes a difference to you. Say you value the significance of Sarita's lover over your pay check."

"It's not about my pay check."

"Isn't it?"

"I don't think I'm willing to quit my job for this. Besides, it wouldn't do any good if I did. I have no control over where we cut."

Emily knew this was true but couldn't find anywhere else to aim. Mason was the only available target for her sudden anger. "All of this is going to be *ruined*. These trees can be considered cultural artifacts. They need to be protected."

"I can't do anything about that."

"Well, *somebody* needs to."

"I understand that this could seriously derail your research—"

"My research? This is bigger than that. We're talking about a culture that is already nearly extinct."

Mason looked at her as they walked. "I know a little something about that."

"What do you...oh, right." The heat rushed her

cheeks. "I'm sorry."

"Not your fault. The Hopi number less than seven thousand. Remember when I mentioned the *Hopituh Shi-nu-mu*? That's us. It means the Peaceful Little Ones. We're dwindling every year. But hundreds of other tribes have vanished altogether. No one speaks their languages anymore. No one prays to their gods."

"That's my point," Emily said. "What we've found here, this story that Sarita's lover is telling us, it may not be very grand in the scheme of things, and it may not even be worth much from a scientific standpoint. But it was the most necessary thing in the world to those two. And if there's a chance that I can save it—"

"There's not. I wish that wasn't true."

They walked in silence.

Emily tried to let go of her frustration, but it held on, making her want to stomp her foot and throw the kind of tantrum worthy of a nine-year-old who was about to have her toys taken away. Is this what Magnelli meant when he said that there was nothing fair in academia? No, it went deeper than that. Having her research shut down wasn't what made her walk with her hands curled into fists. This sense of loss was more difficult to define.

"What if we found the trees first?" Mason asked. "Before the cut? We could record all the symbols before the crew got this far."

"We don't have enough time."

"We could start right now."

She forced a smile that she knew looked artificial. "Thanks for the offer, but at the rate I'm going, it could be a month before I'm certain I've seen everything."

"I want to help. I just don't know what to do."

"How about you chain yourself to a tree and refuse to move?"

"If I thought it would do any good, I'd be the first to give it a try."

Emily realized that he was telling the truth. For a person he barely knew and a shepherd long since dead, he'd take a wild risk like that. "Careful," she said. "I might get desperate enough to take you up on the offer."

They walked on, the forest seeming to grow quieter as they neared the trail where Mason's truck was parked. Emily realized that the best she could do was work as quickly as possible. Maybe she'd get lucky and the shepherd's chosen trees wouldn't pass into the area destined for deforestation. "I'm going to stay until dark," she said. "I want to maximize the daylight. But thanks for letting me know. You didn't have to do that. For that matter, you didn't have to do *any* of this."

"Let me do more. I'll run to Rockerton and bring back dinner. If you're going to be out here until sundown, the least I can do is make sure you're not starving to death."

Emily experienced a moment of uncanny recall. The last time a man had mentioned dinner, Norris Cook, lit professor, had said, *I think it's high time that you and I enjoyed a repast other than that found in the university dining hall.* What kind of dinner invite was that? Emily should've known immediately how the evening was going to unfold.

"Dinner for two," Mason said, looking a little nervous. "We can, uh, eat on the tailgate of the truck. How's that for classy?"

Emily stood in the middle of a forest on the side of

a Colorado mountain, her fingernails dirty and her tears waiting to fall at the thought of losing her precious trees, and this slightly scruffy woodworker with the Indian eyes was offering to bring her something to eat.

"Are you asking me out?"

"Well..." He jammed his hands into his jacket pockets and went from looking nervous to downright uncomfortable. "Sorry, I know this is totally not a good time, and you and I don't exactly have compatible careers or anything."

"*Yes.*"

"Yes?"

"It sounds wonderful. Now get out of here before I change my mind."

He gave her a half smile, turned, and headed for the truck with its company logo on the door, the very company that—come tomorrow—would begin the process of erasing Sarita's lover and the story he was trying to tell.

Chapter Twelve

Halfway through dinner, Mason heard the voice of Jimmy White Cloud as clearly as if the gnarled old man had been squatting on a fallen log only a few feet away: *Life is a wheel, and if you are as patient as the river, the wheel will come back around and give you a second chance.*

Was this his second chance? Ever since the accident many years ago, he'd been afraid of a lot of things, most prominently life itself. Yet here was the wheel, still spinning, still waiting for him to dust himself off.

"...it's not like I'm out here trying to cure cancer or anything," Emily was saying, "but I'm also not one of those doctoral candidates who simply jumps through the hoops in order to get the degree. I enjoy being out here. Except for the bugs, of course."

Mason scooped the last of his ice cream with a plastic spoon. He'd returned from Rockerton with sandwiches, cardboard bowls of soup, and two half-pints of chocolate ice cream. He had no way of knowing if she liked that flavor, but as it turned out, he'd guessed correctly. "I suppose I'll be calling you 'doctor' one of these days."

She wrinkled her nose. "Sounds kind of stuffy, doesn't it?"

"You worked hard. Nothing stuffy about that."

They talked for half an hour after their ice cream was finished, Mason swaying his legs under the tailgate and Emily sitting cross-legged, her shoes in the grass. He hadn't had a conversation like this in...how long had it been? Emily's passion for her work was clear, and when she spoke of Sarita and the nameless man who'd hidden her name in a tree, she didn't seem like an Easterner out of place in the great green wild. She seemed like a woman hunting for the truth of a lost love.

Reluctantly, Mason said he needed to go, and Emily accepted his ride into town, zipping her tent and leaving her campsite for the evening. The fading light made further investigation impractical. Emily's motel room would provide her with the online access she'd need to correspond with her university and type up the latest summary of her research.

"Can I give you a lift up the hill in the morning?" he asked as she climbed from the truck in the motel parking lot.

Her hand on the door frame, she hesitated for a moment, and he wished he could have read her thoughts. "I've already hired Tunny. Thanks, though."

"No problem."

She didn't smile or say goodnight, and Mason hated himself for siding with the enemy; he was a logger, and tomorrow that would put him directly at odds with her. He pulled into the street, drumming his fingers on the wheel.

If Grandpa Jimmy were right and this was his second chance, it picked a hell of a way of presenting itself.

Once he was home, he stood in his garage and

looked around. Usually the scent of wood shavings centered him. Working the boards until they were smooth, passing his hands over their sanded curves—this was his way of making peace with the world, an armistice between him and whatever troubles bothered him that day. But now he felt only a continued restlessness, and his usual place of solitude couldn't alleviate it.

He headed into the house and sought refuge in the shower where he lingered under the spray, letting the hot water sluice down his shoulders and back. If there were an answer in the falling droplets, it eluded him.

Eventually he turned off the water and stepped out. Wrapping a towel around his waist, he wiped the fog from the mirror and studied his chin. Shaving wasn't something he needed to do with regularity; Hopi genes didn't lend themselves to facial hair. But he shaved anyway, more as an act of meditation than anything else. With that done, he cast the towel over the shower-curtain rail and walked naked into his bedroom, which was as dark as a cave.

He made it almost to the bed, then stopped.

What was that?

He held his breath but heard no sound. He was alone, yet something hit the tripwire of his instincts.

Slowly he backed out of the room and studied the doorway. In the dark, the jamb and frame were barely visible, outlining a black rectangle in which lived the red eyes of his alarm clock. Something about that shape...

And then he knew.

"I'll be damned."

He threw on the light and found his jeans and shirt,

hoping Emily would still be awake.

****

Fieldbook open on her chest, head submerged in the thick motel pillow, Emily opened her eyes. Had someone just knocked? In the last minute or so, she must have dozed off, and now she was dreaming that she had a visitor. Maybe it was the maid here to tell her that she'd overslept and that it was time to get her tush out the door so that someone with a vacuum could clean up those crumbs of granola bar she'd dropped on the carpet. She'd given up on the tent and moved into a rented room, but her diet hadn't improved any.

They pounded the door again. This was no dream.

Blinking, Emily swung her legs off the bed, the book tumbling to the floor, its pages fluttering. Was she so emotionally exhausted that sleep had stolen in on her with such speed?

"Emily, it's me."

Mason?

She went to the door, her bare feet nearly tripping over one of her discarded shoes. Wait. She stopped with her hand on the knob. She'd been sleeping and probably looked like it. She didn't want to open the door as the Bride of Frankenstein.

"Emily?"

"Just a sec!"

She looked at the mirror through the bathroom door. Her hair was a three-car pileup, and as she raked her fingers through it, she asked herself why it mattered. She wasn't trying to impress anyone.

Or was she?

Enough. She went back to the door and opened it to find him in mid-knock.

"Hey," he said.

"Uh, hi."

"It's late."

"Yeah."

"Sorry about that. I'm not stalking you or anything."

Emily embraced herself in the chill night air, rubbing her arms against the cold. "If I thought you were a stalker, I wouldn't have left the can of pepper spray back there under my pillow."

"I'll consider myself forewarned." He flashed a quick smile. "I had an epiphany."

"At one in the morning?"

"That's when the best ones always happen."

"You have them often?"

"Not as often as my grandfather. He had all the big medicine. I just have to count on luck. But I know what that circle is supposed to be."

Emily, still tugged-at by sleep, couldn't see where this was going. "Do you want to come in? It's a little cool out here."

"Sure, thanks."

Emily closed the door behind him and conducted a hasty and admittedly belated search for anything she should've picked up before inviting a man into her rented lair. But she saw no bras hanging on doorknobs or panties peeking out of suitcases. Close call.

"I'm talking about the tree," Mason said, taking a seat in the room's single chair.

Emily sat on the edge of the bed. From this angle, she could see herself in the bathroom mirror. Who was that woman? Emily knew no one like that, who slept in the clothes they'd worn in the woods and spent the wee hours chatting with men they'd known for only three days. Surely that was someone else in the glass. "I think my lack of caffeine can account for the fact that I'm not quite sure what you're talking about."

He leaned forward, elbows on his knees. "Sure you do. The shepherd carved a shape that we couldn't recognize. It was sort of like a circle, a circle that was bigger than he was."

"Oh, right." She shook her head, irritated at herself. "I'm usually not this dense."

He looked as excited as a schoolboy. "Forgiven. But I know what that circle is."

"Are you going to make me guess? I'm not a very good guesser at this hour."

"It's a cave."

Emily let that move through her, whispering through her bones like a secret: *cave.*

"I realized it as I was walking through my house in the dark," he continued. "My bedroom felt like a cave. The doorway was pitch black like that. And that's what the shepherd was talking about."

"So that means…"

"There's a cave out there."

Emily shivered not only because of the cold. Caves spoke of hidden things, of treasures secluded in the wilderness, of hiding places for outlaws and shelters for those in a storm.

"I don't suppose," he said, "you've seen anything like that on your maps."

She shook her head. "My laptop is crammed with topographical illustrations of a four-county area. By now I probably know them as well as anyone. I haven't seen or heard of any cave systems around here."

"Me, neither. And I've lived here for a little over ten years."

"Maybe you're wrong. Maybe it's not a cave." She could tell by the look on his face that he was convinced. He *wanted* to be right, and she understood his desire. The thought of a secluded grotto in the trees... "Let's say you're right," she said. "I have two questions."

"Go ahead."

"One, where is it? And two—"

"What's in it?"

She nodded. "Exactly."

Neither of them spoke. They sat staring into each other's eyes, as if they might realize together the answer to these mysteries.

Then Mason said, "I know it's the middle of the night, but would you like some coffee? There's an all-night café about three blocks from here."

Emily looked down at herself. Was she in any kind of condition for an impromptu public appearance? "There's not a dress code, is there?"

"As long as you have shoes and a shirt, I think you'll be okay. And did I mention they have pie?"

"Well, hell. Why didn't you say that in the first place? Key lime speaks louder than words."

"I'll keep that in mind."

She got up and left him smiling, proud of herself for her sudden conversational skills and excited by the thought of sharing coffee in the middle of the night.

She closed the bathroom door behind her, turned on the light, and told the prudent woman in the mirror to get over it: things were changing all around her.

Chapter Thirteen

Emily's morning ride to the campsite cost her twenty dollars and a full tank of gas.

"Never done work for a university before," Tunny said, working the gears of his flatbed truck. "But I'm always glad to lend a hand to folks smarter than me." He grinned, revealing the charming gap between his front teeth.

"I'm sorry it's not more glamorous," she replied, bouncing on the passenger's seat with her fieldbook open in her lap.

"Don't sweat it, ma'am. It's this or sitting around the house, waiting for the mailman to deliver my V.A. disability check. And I'd just spend that on horses and fast women."

Emily smiled and shook her head. She'd arranged Tunny's services before her arrival in Rockerton, contacting him through the Chamber of Commerce. Tunny was the town's resident handyman. He could weld, paint, spit, and hunt with equal skill and knew the area and its residents as well as anyone. He claimed that his second wife had left him to pursue a career in the adult film industry. Since he always said it with a straight face, Emily had yet to decide whether or not he was kidding.

"Gettin' kind of a late start today," the big man observed.

"I guess I ...I didn't get much sleep last night."

"Stay up watchin' old kung-fu movies on the motel TV?"

"Among other things." Actually, she'd spent two hours at the little diner with Mason after he showed up at her room, and she'd consumed so much coffee and sugar that there was no way this side of the Continental Divide that she'd been able to get any more sleep that night. Mason had dropped her off at the motel—walking her to the door—with stars filling the sky overhead. By now, he'd reported to work and resumed the business of cutting down her trees.

"You mind my askin' how it's goin' with the book?"

"The book?"

"You're writin' a book, ain't you? My dad always wanted to write a book. Said he was goin' to write a fishin' book. Mama said he ought to, considering he paid more attention to catfish than he did to her." Tunny chuckled. "I miss 'em both, bless their souls."

"I'm not sure if what I'm doing is book-worthy, but there have been a few interesting developments recently."

"Glad to hear it. If there's one thing this worn-out town needs, it's a good strong shot of *interesting*. In fact, the last time somethin' like that happened was when the principal of our high school got caught writin' erotic stories for the internet. Said he was *blogging*, and damned if I know exactly what that means, but it don't sound kosher, for sure. Or healthy, for that matter..."

Emily heard little of what he said. She thought of the cave. What if the only way to locate the cave was to find more clues in the trees? And what if those trees stood in the section of the forest destined to be razed?

And most importantly, how could she stop it?

When all else fails, depend on the insight of your wrinkled elders.

Magnelli? Could he possibly help? She sometimes heard his voice in her head, offering his flakes of dubious advice, but he had little hope of assisting her with this particular problem. Still, it wouldn't hurt to call, if only to hear his condolences. It was true what they said about misery loving company, even when that company was a seventy-year-old curmudgeonly academic with narcissistic tendencies.

"This close enough?" Tunny asked, driving the nose of his truck into the treeline.

"Perfect." She gathered her things and slid out.

"I'll be back at four," he promised. "You need anything for your camp? Lantern batteries? Bug repellent? Two sticks to rub together for a fire?"

She gave him a quick smile that she didn't really feel. "I'll be okay. Thanks for the lift."

"Hey, it's all that fancy university money that I'm after. Sure beats doin' honest work."

She waved goodbye, and after the sound of his aging transmission faded in the distance, she looked around. The orange flags she'd left yesterday marked the nearest tree she'd found.

Before she could catch herself, she wished Mason were here.

So as to avoid dealing with the implications of that renegade thought, she hurried through the tall grass, touched that first tree, and followed the path she'd memorized to the next. Soon she'd reached the last one she'd found, which was at least fifty yards from the first. Unfortunately, Sarita's lover hadn't chosen his trees with any kind of logic. Or perhaps he had, and Emily had yet to deduce it.

Powering up her GPS unit, she moved farther into the forest. If there were any more marked trees out here—and she trusted that there were—then she would need to race to find them. Though Mason would do his best to slow his team's progress, inevitably they'd make their way to her side of their cutting zone, which meant she needed to push herself.

All that pushing wore her out. Two hours later, having investigated and cataloged dozens of trees, she was deeper in the woods with nothing to show for it.

"And probably covered in ticks by now," she muttered. She slumped down and spent some time with her water bottle.

That's how it went most of the day. Her frustration mounted with every aspen that failed to provide the clues she sought. At some point in the afternoon, the sound of chainsaws carried through the forest.

They were close. Mason's friends worked not far up the hill, drawing nearer with every toppled tree.

Emily forced herself to move even faster, and her body paid the price. By four o'clock she was more than ready to flee. Though she'd originally intended to camp tonight in her tent, a hot bath at the motel room was about the only thing that made sense.

"What's the good word?" Tunny asked as he drove them back down the mountain that afternoon.

"Right now, I'm a woman in need of a cell phone signal."

"Give us another mile or so. Reception usually kicks it up a notch once we're over the next ridge."

He was right. As soon as the bars leaped to life, Emily wasted no time speed-dialing Magnelli. The day had been an utter wash, and every time she thought of the saw blades biting into her trees, she had to bite back a word her mother hadn't taught her.

Magnelli's voice was so abrupt it startled her: "It's war with the Nazi down the hall."

Emily paused and took a breath. The old professor, a man in love with shock value, always started his conversations with the unexpected. "You mean Diederich?"

"No, the ghost of Hitler. Of course I mean Diederich. He's nominated himself for faculty senate."

"And this is bad, why?"

"Oh, I suppose it's not bad at all, my tree-hugging protégé, so long as you have nothing against fascist fools. He's running against *me*, darling. And do you know what makes it even worse?"

She sighed. She didn't have time for her mentor's weird conversational tacks, but she had no choice. The success of her dissertation was tied to his whims. "What's even worse?"

"He's a fan of the New York Mets! I *loathe* the Mets."

"Isn't it cliché to be a Yankees fan?"

He said nothing, then laughed suddenly. "You're right entirely, darling. Of course it is. Still, though, I wish the damned kraut wasn't forcing me actually to *campaign* for the position. You'd think after all these years of sharing the same hall…"

"I need your help."

That stopped him. "Beg your pardon?"

"I have a problem."

"Would that be a problem *grande* or problem *pequeño*?"

"The former."

"Damn. Well, that's why I'm here. They don't give you tenure for nothing. The least I can do is help reduce your mountain to a more manageable molehill."

By now Tunny had delivered her into town. She cupped her hand over the phone and thanked him, then got out at a random intersection. She had no plan for this evening, but for now it didn't matter.

"Are you still there, darling? Lay it on me, as they say."

She told him the story. The loggers. The new area they were about to harvest. The possibility of a cave. She knew she stuttered and rambled, but at least she kept the tears at attention; they wouldn't march down her cheeks without permission. When she was finished, she held the phone to her ear and waited.

Moments passed.

She imagined Magnelli at his desk, toying with an errant thread on his pants.

"Professor?"

"Yes, yes, I'm gathering wool. The doddering elderly among us have the right to stare mindlessly into space as we see fit. You're certain they're coming your way? And who's this Mason fellow, anyway?"

"He's a ...a friend."

"And he's certain of what he's saying?"

"It's *his* crew. They're starting at the eastern edge of their new region or sector or whatever they call it. They're moving west. Toward me."

"And you're convinced there are more messages out there? These *billets doux* the sheep-herder wrote?"

"Yes."

"Would you say these tree-carved pictograms represent an important component of the region's history?"

"Certainly."

"Then your only course of action, clearly, is to get an injunction."

Emily's eyes widened. "An injunction?"

"A legal order that prohibits a particular course of action."

"Yes, I know the meaning of the word. How do I go about getting one? From who?"

"From *whom*. And that would be…let's see…" She heard his chair creak, followed by the rattling of a keyboard. He talked to himself as he worked.

She let him do his thing. Magnelli was at his best when he dug for information, whether it was pottery shards in an Aztec ruin or a pizza joint's number on the back of a newspaper. He was built for research. The same thing could not be said of her.

Her thoughts drifted to Mason. Last night in the coffee shop, they'd talked like old friends who'd happened upon each other after years of being apart. He told her of the books he'd read and of the people he'd left behind on the reservation in Arizona. He made her laugh more than once. At one point she almost asked him about the woman in the photograph, but she steered away from it for fear of what he might say.

Magnelli said something to her, and she forced herself back to the present tense. "I didn't catch that."

"Your *quill*. You do have a pen at hand, I trust?"

"Yes, certainly. Right here." She fished one from her bag and turned to a random blank page in her field book. "Go ahead."

"The Honorable Bailey Daggert."

"A judge?"

"As well as former senior counsel for the Green Sky Legacy."

"Meaning what?"

"It says here that in the days of his private practice, Daggert was an environmental lawyer. Of course, that was twenty years ago…"

"He's here? In this area?"

"Colorado Springs, actually. That's probably a two-hour drive from that bucolic village you currently calling home. How's the cuisine there, by the by? What do those people eat there? Moose burgers?"

"Do you think I have a shot?"

"At eating moose burgers?"

"Professor, please."

"All right, don't get your halo cocked all sideways. Do I think you have a shot? At convincing a judge to issue an order that stops the logging? Hmmm, do you recall the time I foolishly took you and the grad students to the Atlantic City casinos to celebrate our published paper on the Tanzanian diaspora?"

"Of course."

"And do you remember when I drew the king of clubs to win that tiny fortune?"

She just wanted him to get to the point. "Yeah, I remember. You said the odds of that happening under those conditions were almost five hundred to one."

"Precisely. I'd put your odds at close to twice that. Tally-ho, darling," he said and hung up.

Emily looked at the phone, startled to have been so abruptly abandoned. A thousand to one?

She closed her eyes and sighed.

Chapter Fourteen

Mason spent the day wishing he were someone else. Another man. Another job. Doing something other than clearing these trees.

Every time one of the crew approached an aspen, saw in hand, Mason searched it quickly, walking a circle around its trunk and hoping he wouldn't find one of the shepherd's prints etched into it. They asked him what he was doing.

"Safety first," he said. "Just making sure everything's cool before you cut."

But everything was not cool. Everything was, in fact, completely sideways. He didn't know how to convince himself that what he was doing was right. He couldn't figure out how to prevent every tree in this quadrant from falling. And he couldn't stop thinking about Emily.

She was intelligent and unexpected and had no business being out here in the wild, where he'd almost run her over and instead ended up infatuated.

Infatuated? Had he reached that stage already? Removing his hardhat and wiping away a line of sweat, he asked himself to name the last time he'd been infatuated with *anybody*, and he couldn't say.

If he had any guts, he'd sabotage these bulldozers and pour salt into the fuel tanks of every chainsaw in a five-mile radius.

He worked like that throughout the day, clearly agitated and turning surly by noon. He said as little to the crew as possible so as not to give himself away, but he was sure they noticed. The resident Indian had a burr in his saddle, and it was best to leave him alone.

At quarter till five he'd had enough. He radioed the men and told them to put their blades away for the day. No one complained.

Mason got a ride back into town and said little along the way. Everyone knew he hadn't owned a vehicle since the accident on the highway, and when he rode shotgun in silence, they assumed he was thinking about Brianna, whom he'd lost two years ago in a mangle of fire and steel. They were wrong.

"Thanks, man," he said as Allan dropped him off at the corner motel.

"Hey, you doing okay?" Allan asked.

Mason appreciated the honest concern. Allan was the only member of the crew who said grace over his lunch in the afternoon and swore only when absolutely necessary. He and his wife often invited Mason to dinner, and once or twice he'd accepted. "Did you ever want to do anything different for a living?" Mason asked him.

"Different than logging? What else would I do?"

"I don't know. Forget it. Life's a funny thing, that's all."

"Funny good or funny bad?"

"Remains to be seen, I guess. Take it easy." He didn't bother watching the man drive away, but turned and headed for room fourteen. He needed a shower and some quality time with a comb. But he sensed the urgency of the situation. Tomorrow the crew would push even farther west, and though Mason hadn't noticed any of the shepherd's trees today, eventually the saws would find their way.

He ran a hand through his hair. How did he look?

"Cut it out," he whispered to himself. He was acting like a teenager en route to his first date. Mason was an adult with adult priorities, and he had no reason to impress her. They had important business to conduct. Still, a breath mint would've been nice.

He was lifting his hand to knock when she opened the door and said, "I saw you coming."

"I tried to check the trees today."

"And?"

"I didn't see anything. How about you? Any luck?"

"It's like he vanished. Sarita's lover, I mean. I got a headache from looking so hard."

"Can I get your cell number?" He threw it out there before he lost his nerve. The last time he'd asked for a woman's phone number, covered wagons had still been carrying settlers across the Rockies—or so it felt. "It's just easier to get in touch with you, that's all."

She seemed ready to give in to a smile, but it didn't quite touch her lips. "We can trade numbers on the way to the rental agency."

"What are you renting?"

"I need to get to Colorado Springs tomorrow morning. I'm tired of asking the locals to drive me around, yourself included."

"This particular local doesn't mind at all. What's in Colorado Springs?"

"Bailey Daggert."

"Who?"

"A judge whom I hope to sweet-talk into ordering

your company to stay clear of my trees."

Mason absorbed this. Was she serious? Could she actually convince a judge to stop the logging in that quadrant? It didn't sound very feasible, but Mason was currently a man running on faith, and he hadn't run that way for years. "It's over a hundred miles between here and there."

"So my GPS tells me."

"You need any company?"

Again she seemed on the verge of smiling, but she didn't let it show. "I might be gone all day tomorrow, probably leaving at dawn so I can get there as early as possible. I don't know how long these things take. I've never requested a judicial injunction before."

"Maybe I'll take a vacation day. I've got some hours built up."

"Doesn't sound like a very fun way to spend your vacation."

"If you'd rather do this alone, I understand. A woman's got to do what a woman's got to do, right? I can stay here and keep on checking the trees."

After a few silent moments—with Mason feeling the warmth spread in his cheeks—Emily said, "No, I'd like you to come." She looked at the ground, then at the phone in her hand, and anywhere but at him. "But only on one condition."

At this point, Mason couldn't begin to guess what she'd say next. Having only recently admitted his infatuation, and even more recently invited himself on a day trip with the object of that infatuation, he was too nervous to do anything but stand there flatfooted and wait for her to reveal her stipulation.

"When we get back," she said, "we find that cave."

****

... though Sarita's exact identity remains unknown, further investigation of the town records will hopefully provide details of her family.

Lying on her bed that night, Emily clicked SAVE and stared at her laptop's screen. She wished she had more to report other than tree locations, dendroglyph dimensions, and blind speculation. She hoped that a visit to the library's hard copy archives would provide her with information about the woman known only as Sarita, but all of that would be moot if she failed to stop the logging operation. Mason had told her that it would take his crew four more days to work their designated area. Four days until all potential traces of Sarita's lover were gone.

She put her hands back to the keyboard, trying to ignore the sad condition of her fingernails.

The city library, though its holdings are not extensive, maintains a digitized record of all area newspapers, dating back to 1887—according to Leena Moraine, librarian.

What next?

She tapped her tongue against her teeth, waiting for her muse. Did she even *have* a muse? She'd never considered herself particularly creative. She was always more of a fact person, thus she found it difficult to guess what she might discover in the shepherd's cave— if indeed the circular rune represented a cave. Finding no immediate source of inspiration, she typed the first word that came to mind:

Mason.

Interesting. The first word she typed had nothing to do with work at all. What would Freud have to say about that? She liked the way he'd blushed this evening when he offered to join her on her trip to Colorado Springs in the morning. She couldn't remember the last time a man had gotten red in the face because of her.

She spent several minutes thinking of him, daydreaming like the girl who sits in the back of the algebra classroom with a window too near for her own good. Then she shook him off and returned to this business of Bailey Daggert.

Having tracked down the man's number, she'd used her most professorial voice when speaking with his administrative assistant. It was the same voice she used when teaching one of the classes Magnelli passed off on her, the kind of voice that said *I know what I'm talking about* and *Don't piss me off* at the same time. Her students usually did well in her classes. Daggert's secretary also seemed to get the message. She said that the judge was free for twenty minutes in the morning, if Emily could be there by ten o'clock.

Emily confirmed the time, hung up, and wondered what the hell she was supposed to wear.

And now, an hour later, she lay on her motel bed with her computer, her thoughts drifting unproductively between work and a local log-cutter who lived in a cabin and didn't own a car.

She used the backspace key to erase his name one letter at a time. What if her shepherd has possessed such technology? If he'd been able to compose his messages digitally and save them to a flash drive the size of his thumb, what stories would he have told?

Emily opened the file where she'd transcribed his note: *She meets me today at our special place. I will write more later and tell the trees of my Sarita, my love.*

In his original Spanish, he'd misspelled the word *special*, but other than that his grammar was surprisingly accurate, indicating an education that belied his occupation. Details like that were important to her research, as she'd assumed that immigrant herders had received little if any formal schooling. Who had taught him to read and write? An amateur analysis of his penmanship revealed a controlled but not beautiful hand. His words were legible though not elegant.

"Who are you?" she asked, not for the first time.

She closed the laptop and went to the shower, turning on the hot water to a point where the motel's second-rate water heater would surely implode within fifteen minutes. When steam turned the little bathroom into a sauna, she slipped off her clothes and was about to step under the spray when she noticed the mirror over the sink. The hot fog had completely obscured the glass. Impulsively, she went to the mirror and used her finger to write *Who are you?*

She didn't know exactly where she was directing the question. At the shepherd? At Mason? Or at herself?

Not waiting for an answer, she turned away and lost herself under the water.

Chapter Fifteen

Summer rain made its own kind of runes on the windshield.

"We needed this," Mason said in the passenger seat of the rental. "The weeds in my flowerbeds were starting to wither."

"Isn't that a good thing?"

"I love planting, but I hate maintaining. The weeds and I have an arrangement. I agree not to yank them up and they agree not to totally suffocate the flowers."

"That's an interesting gardening philosophy."

"My thumb isn't in any danger of turning green."

"Well, at least you have a place to grow things. I don't even have any grass."

"There's no grass in New Jersey?"

"Not in *my* hunting ground. I live in an apartment. No lawn. No squirrels."

"And you're cool with that?"

She took one hand off the wheel and made a so-so gesture.

"Sometimes you want a yard," he said.

"I have my days."

"But first you have to finish school?"

"The school part is over, thank God. Now I'm just wandering through the dark without a flashlight, hoping I bump into something worth writing about. In the academic world, we call that *all but dissertation*, or

ABD. In my case that stands for Academia is Becoming a Disaster."

"And then what? After the dissertation."

"Fruitless job hunting for entry-level positions at obscure community colleges."

He chuckled. "That makes me feel better."

"My future obscurity amuses you?"

"I completed two years at Arizona State. Between my track achievements and my Indian DNA, they gave me a full ride."

"You were a runner?"

"Cross country. I wasn't Olympic material, but I could handle most of those pale-faces they put me up against."

"As the only pale-face in the car, I won't take offense to that, mainly because I can't run fifty yards to catch a bus without hyperventilating. So why did you drop out? Wait, never mind. That's none of my business…"

"Don't worry about it. It's not classified information or anything. My dad's liver started to go south during my senior year in high school. He died on Valentine's Day a year later. He didn't leave behind any life insurance, so I moved back home to help Mom. It was either that or she was going to lose the house."

Emily chose her next words with care. She was thrilled that he'd shared these details of himself with her; she was surprised by her own eagerness to fill in the blanks of his life. But she didn't want to scare him off by pressing too hard or—heaven forbid—showing too much interest.

Was she interested? *Seriously* interested?

She kept her smile to herself. "I guess things

happen sometimes that we don't predict."

"Oh, it was predicted, all right."

"What do you mean?"

"Jimmy White Cloud claimed he saw it in a vision. Two eagles sitting on a rock. One flies away to seek out new lands beyond the mesa, leaving the other behind, just like my dad passing on and leaving my mother. But that one eagle by herself is weak, and her nest is besieged by predators. So she calls out to Sky Father, and he sends her a storm that drives off those who would destroy her nest. But the storm uses up all its rain in the effort, and so it can't go back to where it came from."

Emily looked at him. His eyes were like dark coals, waiting to burn. "He was your grandfather, right?"

"Yes."

"And you're the storm."

"So it would seem."

Emily drove the next five miles without comment. Beyond the rain-smeared windows, the wooded mountains converged in streams so clear they seem to have been made of molten glass.

"It's just an Indian story," he said after a while.

Though Emily was by training a skeptical person, she was at heart a believer. The anthropologist in her saw the cultural value of the grandfather's metaphor, but the woman saw the truth in it.

"What brought you to Colorado?" she asked, more softly than before.

"My mother followed my dad and crossed over to the other side when I was twenty-four, almost ten years ago. I left the day of the funeral, with nothing in my car but a sleeping bag, two books of bad poetry, and a *kachina* doll that Jimmy gave me."

Emily was distantly aware of the word's meaning. "A *kachina* is a spirit, right?"

"Sort of. Jimmy used the term *qatsina*. It represents a dancer who's imitating a particular spirit. In this case, that spirit is the storm."

"You."

"More or less."

I'm riding in the car with a storm, she thought.

"This is our exit," Mason said, and a moment later the GPS confirmed it.

Emily slowed and keyed her turn signal. "But why Rockerton? There doesn't seem to be much there but a couple of diners and a lot of stray dogs."

"Have you heard them barking?"

"Just outside my motel window, unfortunately."

"Our so-called animal control officer got fired last month for accidentally tagging and bagging a cat that belonged to the mayor's wife."

"Ah, small-town drama."

"At its finest."

Emily exited the highway and approached Colorado Springs. Roadside signs boasted of the Air Force Academy and the efficiency of the Mountain Metropolitan Transit.

"Do we know where we're going?" Mason asked.

"Nobody knows where we're going these days. That's why we have satellites." She followed the directions on the device's little screen, and a block later she realized that Mason had never answered the question about why he'd left his home and ended up in Rockerton. Had he intentionally sidestepped the issue, not wanting to discuss it?

She wanted to ask but talked herself out of it. The day was going too well to potentially spoil it by digging too deeply. Like Sarita's lover, Mason would either reveal his secrets in his own time or cloister them away forever.

By the time they reached the judicial building, the rain had all but given up. Emily got out of the car and felt a few last drops on her face, like goodbye kisses. The clouds had started to pull apart. By noon she expected the sun.

But between now and then, she expected a whole lot more. Like a sympathetic judge, for starters. And at least a little bit of luck.

"Do we have a plan?" he asked as they converged on the sidewalk. He wore neatly pressed khakis and a white shirt, the sleeves rolled up to reveal his brown forearms. A pale blue stone on a leather string lay in the hollow of his throat. "Or are we just depending on your feminine charm?"

"If that's the case, then we're probably in trouble. I don't think my charms will get us very far. Those things get rusty if you don't use them, you know."

She led the way toward the judicial building and said thanks when Mason opened the door for her. It was nice being out with a man, even if they weren't really *out* as in dinner but only *out* as in somewhere away from her motel room.

The lobby smelled of lemon-scented cleaner. The tile floor had been recently waxed. Emily approached the first official-looking person she saw, asked for directions, and eventually learned that Bailey Daggert's office was on the second floor. She chose the stairs instead of the elevator—her recently thirty-year-old bod needed the exercise—and took a seat beside Mason on a small sofa when Daggert's administrative assistant offered it.

She looked down at the thin folder of papers on her lap. Was it *too* thin? Would a more impressive stack of documentation convince him that her cause was legitimate?

"I'm more than just a tree-hugger," she whispered.

Mason leaned toward her. "Excuse me?"

"I'm not some crazy environmentalist with an axe to grind."

"I hope that's not going to be the argument you're using with the judge."

"What, you don't find me convincing?"

"Honestly, I thought you *were* crazy. Why else would you be stumbling around in the woods, waiting for me to come along and run you over?"

She poked him on the leg. "I wasn't stumbling."

He spread his hands wide. "Hey, I'm just saying."

The secretary interrupted them. "Ma'am? Judge Daggert will see you now. Through that door, please."

"Here we go," Emily said as she stood, pressing the wrinkles from the pantsuit she'd chosen this morning. Was gray too severe? Would she come across as bland? And what about her shoes?

"I'll stay," he said. "You don't need me in there."

"Are you sure?"

"Just go do your thing. I'll be all right. Plenty of month-old magazines to read." He grabbed one from the top of the stack. "Break a leg."

Emily wasn't sure if that was an appropriate blessing for anyone outside the theater business, but she'd take what she could get. Clasping the folder under her arm, she nodded a thank-you at the secretary and passed through a door marked PRIVATE.

Just before the door closed, she looked back.

Mason caught her eye and winked.

Chapter Sixteen

Bailey Daggert swung the silver club, his expensive sport coat bunching at the shoulders.

Emily watched the putter make contact with the ball, which in turn drew a line across the carpet and vanished into a cup on the far side of the room.

Emily looked from the cup to Daggert's face. For a moment he seemed concerned only with the success of his shot, as if by committing its trajectory to memory, he could recreate it on the course. He looked younger than his fifty-one years, with the features of a Roman senator and the kind of cold blue eyes she might have fallen for in the days of her youth, like a gypsy girl chasing after a magic charm.

He caught her watching him. "Three shots between each appearance on the bench."

She wasn't sure what that meant. "Pardon me?"

He crossed the room, moving like a man who spent time at the gym. "Docket's as busy as all hell. My breaks last only as long as it takes to sink three puts. That's number one." He bent down and retrieved his ball, tossed it, and caught it.

"I see."

"Shut the door, please."

Emily did as she was asked.

Daggert placed the ball on the opposite side of his office and wiped a speck of lint from his captoe shoe.

"To what do I owe the pleasure, miss . ?"

"I'm Emily Radsco, from the univer—"

"Hold that thought." He drew the putter back, paused, and swung.

The ball rolled wide of its mark by an inch.

The veins in the backs of his hands bulged as he clenched the putter. Emily expected a curse, but instead he looked up, grinning. "There's a reason a man should never try to sink a twelve-footer in the presence of a beautiful woman."

She smiled politely. "I don't want to take up too much of your time, Your Honor."

"It's Bailey, please." He stepped toward her and offered his hand. "There's no 'your honor' around me unless you're groveling for the court's mercy."

Emily knew that assessment wasn't far from the mark. "I appreciate your seeing me on such short notice."

"Evidently you assume that judges lead eventful lives. For the most part, it's paperwork and monotony. Have a seat." He motioned to a pair of small sofas. A series of photos hung on the wall, featuring Daggert in ski gear, snorkeling gear, and deep-sea-fishing gear. He was clearly a man fond of expensive equipment. He waited until Emily had chosen a seat, then dropped down with the putter across his knees. "Do you drink coffee?"

"I'm fine, thank you."

He gave her his full attention, which surprised her. Emily had been expecting an uninterested, overworked old man who read dusty legal briefs while listening to her with only one ear. But he seemed to care only for what she was about to say.

And what *was* she about to say?

"I was hoping to speak to you concerning some research I've been conducting as part of my dissertation."

"Dissertation? If that's what you're up against, Emily—may I call you Emily?—then you have my full condolences." He laughed to let her know he was kidding; he had one of those laughs designed to carry across a cocktail lounge. "You and I both know that there's nothing more pointless in the world than the pursuit of the celebrated doctoral degree."

"It feels that way on some days."

"Come on, honestly. A colleague of mine just concluded six years of studying Shakespeare's navel lint just so he could teach for a pittance at Pikes Peak Community College. At least in the law field, the juris doctorate can snag you a fancy black robe." He pointed to his, which hung from the back of his door beside a Denver Broncos ball cap. "Other than that, it's overrated."

"You're probably right."

"Am I talking too much?" he asked.

"You're fine."

"I do that when I'm nervous."

"I...don't think you have any reason to be..."

"Sure I have," he said. "Most of the people who walk into this office are certified codgers. You know the kind? Card-carrying old grumblers, each uglier than the last. Right now, I feel like a gumshoe in an old detective film when the *femme fatale* struts through his door."

"I don't know about *that*, but I certainly didn't mean to strut." She didn't know what else to say. This conversation was definitely *not* unfolding as she'd envisioned.

Daggert smiled. "My apologies. Please, proceed."

Here we go. Eyes to the front of the class.

"Call me a symbologist," Emily began. She told him of her training and of her trade, of convincing her mentor of the validity of her project, of finding that first dendroglyph concealed in the trees. She delivered the speech mostly from memory, and the wonderful thing was that he honestly seemed to be listening. She noticed when he glanced down at her left hand. *No,* she thought, *I'm not married but please listen to what I'm saying; hearts depend on this.*

When she was finished, she gave a little wave. "So…that's it. That's my story. I'm here because I think those trees have high historical value and are deserving of preservation, at least until I can ensure I've recorded all the carvings." With all of that said, she waited.

He leaned forward, a captain on the prow of his ship. "Would you have dinner with me?"

Of all the things he might have uttered in response to her brief presentation, this was the only one for which she hadn't prepared a response. It came with neither context nor preamble. Emily had spent the last six minutes delivering her own personal Gettysburg Address, and what did she get in return?

"I don't mean to belittle what you're saying," Daggert explained. "The talk in the country-club locker room is that I have a soft spot for the environment. It's true. I drive an electric car, a Tesla. The fact of the matter is that maybe I can help you and maybe I can't. But I hope we can discuss it over four courses of the finest vegetarian food you can find in the city. What do you say?"

Emily blinked three times. She suddenly felt like a woman underwater, one who'd come unequipped for the experience. "I'm flattered but—"

"I don't invite every woman out the moment she walks through my office door, I can assure you." He gave a lord-of-the-manor laugh. "But there's something about you that intrigues me. You say there's some endangered history in the area, and that worries me. I want to look further into it. But quite frankly, I'd also like to get to know you better."

Emily thought of Mason. Every time she woke up last night in her somewhat uncomfortable motel bed, she'd replayed those moments with him. It was exciting to be interested in someone, to flirt with them, to anticipate seeing them again. Daggert's abrupt proposal felt like an interruption.

"You're not saying anything," he observed. "Can I infer that I've taken your breath away?" Never letting go of his smile, he glanced at his watch. "Listen. I need to get back to the grind. But I'm serious about the date. Call it meeting me halfway. You tell me more about this farmer of yours—"

"Shepherd."

"Right, shepherd. You tell me all the details, we can get to know each other, and maybe we'll both end up enjoying ourselves. I know it's sudden, but some of the best things in life start out that way, right?"

Emily wondered if sitting down to dinner with this man was required in order to get the injunction against the loggers. Daggert didn't strike her as a man who gave without getting something in return.

"Well?"

What could she do? Did she have any other choice? If she said no, would she be able to locate another sympathetic judge in time to save her trees?

She nodded slightly. "That would be...acceptable."

"Excellent!" He stood up. "I'll call you later this afternoon after the docket's had its wicked way with me. Do you have a card?"

A card? Emily was so jolted by the dinner invitation that it took her a moment to figure out what he was saying. "I...don't have a business card. Here." She printed her number on the corner of a page in her fieldbook, tore it off, and handed it to him as she stood.

"It's been very nice meeting you," Daggert said. "You've got a hell of a story, and I'm anxious to hear more about it tonight."

Emily felt as if she'd just been cornered, and now all she wanted was to escape. She had to get out of here before she told this man that the deal was off. "I'll see you then." She pointed herself toward the door, hoping she felt more composed than she looked.

"Looking forward to it!"

She reached for the doorknob and freed herself from the office, feeling as if she'd somehow betrayed Mason by accepting Daggert's offer.

In the waiting area, Mason put down his magazine and stood. "How did it go?"

She didn't know what to say. She walked by him without speaking.

"Emily, what's wrong?"

She kept walking. She needed to see the sun.

****

The sky defeated her.

After feeling trapped underwater, Emily had wanted to experience the sun on her face. But the clouds remained, stitched in a gray tapestry that hung low over the city. At least it was no longer raining.

He touched her elbow tentatively, as if afraid of her reaction. "Hey."

On the sidewalk in front of the judicial building, she turned to him. "He said he'd listen to me, okay?"

"What's that mean? You weren't in there very long."

"He said he's an environmentalist."

"Well, that's good, right?"

She looked down at her notes just so her eyes wouldn't give her away. "He wants to talk to me about it more tonight."

"Then why do you look like you're about to punch somebody in the face?"

Emily hesitated, frustrated with herself and with Daggert and even with Mason for working for the company that was a day or two away from cutting down everything that mattered to her.

Enough with the tantrum, Magnelli said. *Man up, for God's sake.*

Emily met Mason's gaze. "He told me he'd consider it over dinner."

"What? He asked you out?"

"There wasn't really anything I could—"

"He hit on you?"

"It wasn't like that, all right? Was he a little aggressive? Sure. But did he do or say anything inappropriate? Not really."

"And you said yes?"

This was the hard part. "I…I don't think I had a

choice, not if I want him to consider issuing an order to stop the logging."

Mason nodded. That nod could have meant anything. Was it a nod to say that he understood? A nod of resignation?

"He wasn't a creep or anything," she said. "At least not much."

"Hey, it's cool."

"Is it?"

He shrugged with one shoulder. "Sure, whatever."

Emily considered him. She was in no mood for petulant shrugs, but at the same time, his body language implied something nice: He didn't want her to go out with the judge.

She didn't press him. "If we stand here long enough, we're probably going to get rained on. So if you don't want to see how frizzy and awful my hair becomes under those conditions, I suggest we get ourselves into the car and then to the nearest coffee shop. You can be mad at me later."

"Who said I was mad?"

Emily gave him a grin to let him know that she knew better, then headed to the rental.

When Mason dropped onto the passenger's seat and closed his door, he said, "One thing is for sure. I never thought I'd be using my vacation days this way."

"You'd rather be on a beach in Aruba than following me on a wild goose chase?"

"I'm not much of a beach guy. And besides, I've always had a thing for wild geese."

"Lucky for me."

Chapter Seventeen

Mason Hitapwa, grandson of a prophet and seer, never felt more Indian than when he stood in the middle of a shopping mall. He turned a complete circle, surrounded by dozens of shops that sold things no one really needed yet everyone wanted. Two centuries ago this had been Cheyenne and Arapaho land. Those ancient people would have looked at this place and thought it was the land of spirits, where nothing was as it seemed.

"And they'd be right," he said to himself.

After their lunch of mall pizza, Emily had excused herself and vanished into the ladies' room, leaving Mason alone with his thoughts, which today seemed a dangerous thing to do. He liked being with her even when they were doing nothing at all, just browsing the stores and watching their shared reflection in the glass. And now he thought about where she'd be this evening—enjoying a meal that probably cost as much as he made in a week.

He scowled at himself and then slurped his soda through his straw. When was the last time he'd actually felt *jealous*?

"Something funny?"

Startled, he stabbed himself in the roof his mouth with the straw.

"Sorry," Emily said, not looking very sorry.

He smiled and wiped his lips. "Don't sneak up on a guy like that."

"I thought you were looking a little overwhelmed."

"Shopping malls do that to me."

"Shopping malls do that to *everyone*."

"We've been here for over two hours and have nothing to show for it but pizza stains."

"Doctoral candidates are kind of like starving artists," she explained. "We come to malls mainly for people watching. I can't afford a sixty-dollar pair of jeans."

"We still have a lot of time to kill," he said, almost adding *before your date tonight.*

"We *should* be spending that time searching for more evidence of Sarita's lover."

Mason shook his head. "By the time we made it back, we'd just have to turn around again. Come on. There's got to be something in this city that can occupy two people on a budget."

They'd parked at the opposite end of the mall, which meant their return trip took them past the same windows full of mannequins far trendier than real people. The clothing displays prompted Mason to say, "You know, I was once commissioned to design a wooden wardrobe for a woman in a wheelchair."

"Sounds like a challenge."

"She wanted shoe nooks in both doors, and the interior hanger bar needed to roll outward, sort of like a desk drawer."

"Okay, that sounds like *more* than a challenge."

"I'm good with wood, but with moving parts...not so much."

"So it didn't work out?"

"It worked fine. As long as there weren't any clothes on the rack."

"Uh-oh."

"Yeah, when there were clothes hanging on the bar, all of that weight tipped the whole thing over whenever it was rolled out."

Emily smiled. "Sounds like your wardrobe wasn't exactly handicap accessible."

"I could have murdered the poor woman with that thing. Good thing she wasn't around for the test drive that almost flattened me."

"So what did you do?"

"Lit it on fire and watched it burn in my backyard."

She looked at him, eyes wide.

"Just kidding. I told her that the only way it was going to work is if I bolted it to her bedroom wall. I'll never forget what she said to me. 'I live in a world of wheels, Mr. Hitapwa. Everything moves. It will be nice to have something finally permanent.'"

"That sounds rather profound."

"I thought the same thing. Still do."

They eventually located the car, and they spent the remainder of the afternoon touring the city. Mason—who visited here occasionally—showed her the city parks, a sculpture gallery, and a custom furniture store where one of his china cabinets was on display. He got a kick out of making her laugh, and more than once he caught himself staring at her. He waited for his grandfather to speak up and offer some advice, but Jimmy White Cloud's wisdom went only so far; the ways of women eluded even Hopi medicine men.

It all ended when her phone rang." That must be him," she said.

With Mason listening to one side of the conversation, Emily made arrangements to meet at a restaurant called the Penrose Room. The hardest thing he'd done in a very long time was to drive her to that appointment. Except it wasn't an appointment.

It was a date.

He pulled up at the restaurant twenty minutes later, gripping the wheel with both hands.

"Hey," she said.

He looked over at her.

"This is no big deal."

"You don't have to explain it to me."

"And you don't have to act like you don't care." She reached over and—very briefly—touched his arm. "I had a really good time with you today."

"Thanks."

"And the day's not over yet. I just have this one thing to do."

She was right. He was being an asshole. This was just business, after all, and her business was the preservation of those trees. "Give him hell."

She smiled. "Will do." She checked herself once in the mirror on the back of the visor, and was gone.

Mason put the car in gear and drove away, still smelling her perfume.

****

Emily entered the restaurant wearing her most durable armor. When it came time to defend her dissertation one of these days, she expected to feel this same way, as if danger lurked in innocent places, waiting to take her down.

She saw Daggert across the room, surrounded by the slightly overstated elegance of the dining area. A carpeted dais on one side supported a baby grand piano, though the musicians had yet to take up their instruments.

And the day's not over yet, she'd told Mason moments ago. What had she meant by that?

She didn't know. It was best not to plan too far ahead. Before she could see Mason again this evening, she had to survive this dinner. And this man.

He stood up when he noticed her, perfect in his two-button suit. His white shirt cuffs extended exactly a quarter-inch beyond his coat sleeves, and his pant legs broke across his shoes with tailored precision. His tie was not so conservative, as colorfully daring as an artist's palette.

As he helped her with her chair, he said, "I need to start by apologizing."

"What on earth for?"

He glided around the table and took his seat across from her. "You came to my office for professional help, and I made it sound like singles' night in the judge's chambers. That's not the message I usually send to visitors."

"Not at all. It's fine."

"You're hungry, I hope?" He was probably twenty years her senior, but he was one of those men who'd managed to wrestle age into something of an amicable compromise. Though his hair was the shade of brushed steel, the rest of him belied his age. Emily knew he was a regular at a trendy local gym. She would've put money on it. "I haven't eaten here in months, but I pulled a string or two and got us in on short notice."

Emily thought about the evening she'd spent at the faculty cocktail party last spring. A senator was in attendance, and everyone was vying for his eye in their tuxedos and gowns. Magnelli had sent Emily in his stead, and she spent four hours trying to hold her smile in place while wearing uncomfortable shoes. As she looked around the restaurant, those feelings crept back on her, little thieves trying to steal her courage.

"...so I took the liberty of selecting a wine," Daggert said. "You're not going to break my heart and tell me you're a teetotaler, are you?"

Again with the smile that felt stitched to her face. "I've certainly never been accused of that."

The waiter soundlessly appeared, beaming down on them and going through a litany of vintages that Emily only partially heard. She pictured Mason walking through the trees, his black eyes searching the bark.

Daggert made his selections from the menu, and Emily managed to do the same, and ten minutes later she found herself carrying on mindless conversation about her work and his work and everything else except what mattered to her most. Daggert was clearly interested in her, and there was a time in her life when Emily wouldn't have been immune to his orchestrated charm. She'd been a different woman then, one without a sense of self, giving her body to whatever gladiator happened to win the day.

"And your family?" he asked in between bites of his carrot and ginger ravioli.

"No family."

"Everyone has a family. Unless you were raised by wolves."

She gave him another of her business smiles— more polite than authentic—and shook her head. "Nothing as exciting as wolves. My father left when I was very young. I don't really even remember him. My mother...came and went."

"I'm sorry to hear it. You seem particularly successful for someone who apparently grew up without much of a foundation."

"I got lucky, I guess." That was truer than she cared to admit. Her mother was a child of the 70s who never grew out of her destructive affair with LSD, and she'd bequeathed to her only child a penchant for falling in with the wrong crowd. *Make love, not war, baby*, she'd said to Emily, her bumper-sticker philosophy evidenced in her lifestyle. For a while, Emily had followed a similar path, but now...

"You're drifting," Daggert observed.

"I'm sorry. It's just...I'm really worried that a good chunk of my research is going to be lost."

"So it's to business, then?" He dabbed his mouth with a napkin. "Well, then. The state has granted me the authority to make those kinds of decisions. And I have a soft spot for every green cause that happens down the block."

"I hear a 'but' coming."

"*But* I'm going to need to see it for myself."

"I'm not sure I understand."

"These historic markings, these—what did you call them?"

"Dendroglyphs."

"Exactly. Dendroglyphs. A terrific word." He leaned forward. "I need to see them."

A candle burned on the table between them. Emily didn't like the intimacy it implied. "I'm not really sure if that's possible."

"Of course it is. These markings, these

dendroglyphs are out there, yes?"

"Yes."

"Then prove it. Show me. It's not that I don't believe you. Not at all. But I want to be able to say that I've tromped out there in the briars and seen this history first-hand. Then I'll be in more of a position to make an informed decision."

"I see your point." The last place Emily wanted this man was in the middle of the story she shared with Mason. Somehow, the shepherd's tale had become *their* tale, and to have Daggert wading around in the middle of it…

"How's tomorrow sound?"

Emily leaned back a little. Daggert was handsome and aggressive and his Tesla probably cost more than Emily would ever make in a year. He had great taste in food, spent his summers in the Vermont countryside, and yet here was silly Emily Radsco, trying to find some way to tell him no.

"I can clear my schedule," he said. "We could call it a picnic. You might find this hard to believe, but I happen to own a picnic basket."

"I really don't have a lot of time left before the logging company gets too close."

"All the more reason I should pay a visit as soon as possible. I've been through Rockerton once or twice. I can find my way. Is nine in the morning too early?"

Emily didn't see any way out of it. She could always try a different judge, but instinct warned her that Daggert might undermine her if he heard she was seeking an injunction from another office. Word probably traveled quickly in those circles. This was perhaps only shot at protecting what Sarita's lover had left behind.

"Nine-thirty?" Daggert suggested.

"Nine is fine," she said, still safe behind her smile. "Call me when you're getting close to town, and we can meet. Maybe I'll even spring for breakfast."

He grinned. "Best offer I've heard in ages."

Emily returned to her dinner, and the conversation moved on. She performed a balancing act for the rest of the evening, managing to sound enthusiastic even when she was preoccupied with thoughts of a Hopi wood carver who was likely the last person in North America who still bought poetry books and actually read them. What would he say when he heard that she'd agreed to show Daggert the trees?

"More chardonnay?" Daggert asked.

"Are you trying to get me tipsy, Your Honor?"

"Will it help?"

"Actually," she said, raising the glass to her lips, "it sounds like just what I need."

She sought refuge in the wine but found no peace.

Chapter Eighteen

Mason counted the stars and got as high as seventeen before Emily said, "I had no choice."

Sitting in the passenger's seat of the rental car after dinner, he kept his eyes on the sky overhead. He was relieved when she hadn't asked him if he wanted to drive. Other than taking the company truck between work and home, the only driving he'd done was this afternoon's tour of Colorado Springs, during which he'd never taken the speedometer above forty. Ever since he'd lost Brianna, he stayed off the highways, especially at night.

"Now you're ignoring me?" she asked.

"Do you think we're putting the right people into space?"

"You're not very subtle when it comes to changing the subject, are you?"

"Think about it. Everyone who goes up there, with the exception of the billionaires who buy their way up, is a scientist or an engineer or a planetary physicist."

"That doesn't make sense to you?"

"To some extent, sure. We need those folks to conduct whatever experiments need conducting. But what about composers?"

"Music composers?"

"Or artists. Or playwrights. We need somebody who can tell us what it's like, how it sounds and smells, how it feels to be a human up there between the stars."

"I'm not sure I'm qualified to answer that. But it's a good thought."

He finally turned away from the window and looked at her. In the dark, her face was only partially revealed in the dashboard glow. "Don't take this the wrong way, but I'm very glad I almost ran over you."

She smiled. "Thanks. I think."

"I want to do whatever it takes to keep this story safe, and I want to find that cave."

"Me, too."

"So I'm glad the judge is coming. If I were him, I'd have done the same thing."

"The man's using a picnic as a pretext for hanging out with me."

"Can't say I blame him. I've been making up reasons to do the same thing." There, it was out. He hadn't planned to reveal that much of himself, but the damn stars were just too insistent. "I can't skip work again tomorrow, but I wish I could. I want to help you find this shepherd. I want to know everything he has to say. Before you came along…before you came along, I either went home after work and read myself to sleep or played Texas Hold 'Em at the Cross Cut with guys who think I'm a crazy loner who smokes marijuana in a peace pipe."

"So you're *not* a crazy loner?" She grinned.

"I prefer the term *independent*."

"How about *hermit*?"

"Hopefully it's not as bad as that."

"It takes one to know one. You might have noticed that I haven't met a whole lot of people since I've been in town. No one's lining up to bring me a pie and invite me to the Baptist church."

"So what you're saying is that we're birds of a feather?"

"Flocking together."

He smiled secretly to himself. Flocking together sounded nice. And so he decided to test the limits of his luck. "Can I ask you a question?"

"Do I have to answer honestly?"

"Only if you want."

"I accept those conditions. Go ahead."

Mason chose his words carefully and realized he was nervous. She made him feel that way— simultaneously off balance and at ease. He knew he didn't have much to offer her that a man like Bailey Daggert couldn't surpass. Mason worked a blue-collar routine and didn't even own a vehicle. Daggert probably got Christmas cards from the governor. But sitting here in the car with her tonight…

"You're not asking your question," Emily said.

To hell with it. He looked at her and said, "Are you moving back to New Jersey after this is all over?"

"Depends on the data."

"What do you mean?"

"If I end up with a lot of good research, enough to make a foundation for my dissertation, then yes, I'll return to the university and resume my teaching duties. But if I have insufficient data, then going back means facing the glare of my advisor. And believe me, Medusa has nothing on Dr. Frank Magnelli when it comes to turning people to stone by looking at them."

Mason had known the answer before asking, but that didn't make hearing it any easier. Funny, to finally meet someone extraordinary only to have them fly sixteen-hundred miles away. "He sounds . . . formidable."

"Magnelli? Yeah, he can be the Creature from the Academic Black Lagoon. But he's also sort of my surrogate father, so I cut him some slack." She seemed about to elaborate, but then checked herself and glanced at Mason in the dark. "If it makes any difference, I'm not in a hurry to leave."

He released the breath he'd been holding. Did she feel the same way he did? For that matter, how *did* Mason feel about her? He'd yet to take inventory of his emotions. "Once we convince them not to cut too close to the shepherd's trees, we can take our time looking for any more messages."

"Sounds good."

Mason swung his attention back to the stars. It was safer there. Looking at Emily stirred up too many thoughts that would only end up hurting him in the end. He'd never been one to kid himself, so sitting there with his eyes on the Milky Way, he understood two things. One, this woman who was like no other was going to disappear when her work here was done, and two, she was spending the better part of tomorrow morning with a man who might just have the power and money and charm to win her heart.

Chapter Nineteen

In the morning, Emily awoke in a bed not her own, staring at a water stain in the shape of Mona Lisa.

Tangled in the motel sheets, she stared at the ceiling and wondered what made good old Mona smile like that. Though Emily's freshman humanities instructor had claimed the famous smile was one of calculated indifference, lying here in a state of semi-sleep, Emily disagreed. It looked like Mona was angry at her man and putting on a false face. Or maybe the woman was wearing the wrong shoes or riding out Renaissance-era PMS. Whatever the reason, Mona suffered in silence, as women had been doing since the beginning.

"Good morning," Emily said to her.

She received no response.

"Fine. It's too early for girl talk, anyway." She rolled out of bed and took three steps toward the bathroom before hearing Mason's words again: *Are you moving back to New Jersey after this is all over?* The question sounded innocent but Emily hoped it wasn't. It sounded like one new friend chatting with another. It sounded like he was just being polite. Or, if you were in the mood to torture yourself with foolish notions—as Emily presently was—it sounded like he didn't want her to go.

They'd talked last night for an hour in this very

room after returning from Colorado Springs. He'd been a gentleman and said goodnight at a reasonable hour, which was probably for the best, as Emily had been feeling fairly unreasonable.

"Enough." She banished these thoughts and occupied herself with a toothbrush and the vitamins she'd been taking daily since remaking herself as a responsible adult. These days it felt like a lifetime ago that she'd partied all night on the Jersey Shore with shirtless sitar players and not worried about waking up until noon the next day. The vitamins were confirmation that she'd finally grown up.

She spit into the sink, unconvinced that growing up was worth it.

By the time she showered and made sense of her disagreeable hair, it was almost nine o'clock. By now Mason was at work, perhaps using a chainsaw on a tree that he'd just inspected for the shepherd's mark. Or maybe he was chaining fallen logs to the trailer of an eighteen-wheeler, or sipping coffee and thinking of her.

She frowned at herself and located her shoes. What did it mean if her thoughts turned to him every six and a half minutes? She recalled something Magnelli once said: "Romance is a pain in the ass."

Mona Lisa would probably agree.

Emily laced up the shoes she'd bought specifically for this trip, and then her phone rang.

She scooped it up and recognized the number, even though she'd seen it only once before. The Honorable Bailey Daggert was calling to say he was on his way.

As she spoke with him, her eyes strayed again to the ceiling. But now she saw only an unrecognizable stain. Emily ended the call with a "See you soon!" that sounded more enthusiastic than she felt, then she found a light jacket and waited for him to arrive.

He's not all bad, you know. He happens to be successful and influential, and did I mention he drives a Tesla?

"Whatever." Emily refused to carry on a conversation with herself, and so she reviewed her notes for the next ten minutes until she heard his car pull up outside.

She glanced into the bathroom for a check in the mirror, then opened the door.

"I called the weatherman!" Daggert announced as he sprang from his car. "He promised no rain this morning."

The smile came to Emily's face automatically. "And what did you have to give him in return?"

"Nothing at all. An honest judge never makes back-alley deals."

"And you're an honest judge?"

"So far."

She allowed him to open the passenger's door for her. "So far?"

"Maybe I'm just waiting for an offer I can't refuse." He closed the door and swung around the front of the car. Emily watched him. He wore crisp khakis and a checked shirt straight from a designer outdoorsman's catalog. She tried to imagine how his house was decorated. He looked like a racquetball guy. And he certainly had a huge TV.

He slid behind the space-age steering wheel. "So, navigator, where are we going?"

Emily gave him directions to the secluded track that led up the mountain, then warned, "Your car might get a little muddy."

"All toward a good cause."

"I hope."

"I have our picnic makings in the trunk. But if you don't care for potato salad and fresh fruit, I may be forced into an anxiety attack, because other than champagne, that's all I brought."

"You've never had an anxiety attack."

He threw her a glance. "What makes you so sure?"

"I get the feeling your job requires someone fairly resistant to stress."

"True enough, but I wasn't always the black-robed man in the big chair. If you can believe it, I majored in theater as an undergrad."

"You're right. I *don't* believe it."

He laughed, a healthy baritone sound that filled the car. "No, seriously! I was gang busters as Mortimer Brewster in *Arsenic and Old Lace*, but *Oklahoma!* was my indication that I wasn't cut out for Broadway. I clearly lacked one particular ability required for participation in a successful musical."

Emily took a guess: "You can't sing?"

"Not a single damn note."

She suppressed a giggle. "Not at all?"

"Screeching cats clear the fences when they hear me doing Sinatra."

"That *would* be an impediment in certain careers."

"Indeed. But that didn't stop me from trying out for roles that didn't require golden pipes. And every night just before the curtain went up, the assistant stage manager would take bets on whether or not I was going to vomit with stage fright. So don't be so sure when you assume I've never wanted to wet myself in anxiety."

"I stand corrected. Or *sit*, as the case may be." At that moment, Emily realized the day was actually starting out nicely, and this surprised her. She didn't want to like this man, yet here she was, finding him at least a little bit charming.

They pulled over in a weedy area that was by now well-traveled. Emily had marked this spot with small plastic flags and colored tape.

"Looks like a crime scene," Daggert said.

"Actually, that's a fairly accurate comparison. What I'm doing out here is similar to a criminal investigator. There's a lot of crawling around on the ground and staring at tiny details until your eyes start to cross."

"It's all interesting as hell, if you ask me. It reminds me of how boring my occupation is."

"Should've stayed in the theater."

"You know"—he put the car in park and opened his door—"I think that very thing more often than anyone knows."

Emily showed him the first tree she'd discovered, explaining the history of the Spanish immigrants and what details she knew of the region's status quo at the turn of the twentieth century. Daggert observed it without comment, filing it away with clinical efficiency. He didn't ask questions, and by the third tree it was clear that his interest went only so far as the dendroglyphs concerned him professionally. He wondered aloud if this were ample evidence to warrant a moratorium on logging in the area. "How many trees have you found that are inscribed like this?"

"Four."

He stared down at the barely discernable image of

what Mason asserted was a cave. "Four is a little on the low side. When you initially described the situation, I was envisioning something a bit more…abundant."

Emily wasn't sure what to say. Four or four hundred, what did it matter? A man had once worked here and loved a woman named Sarita. Wasn't that enough?

"What about other evidence?" Daggert asked. "Do you have any bone fragments, bits of broken pots, that kind of thing?"

"I have a…" She stopped before revealing the message they'd found inside the aspen's trunk. Why was she hesitant to tell him? "There's nothing like that."

"That's too bad."

"These carvings are over a hundred years old."

"I understand. But the loggers will say we can just cut out those particular sections of the trunks and let you take them back to your lab. I'm not sure we can make a case for a full-blown stoppage."

"But there could be more of them out here."

Daggert turned and stared into the woods. The green leaves were dotted with the yellows and reds of wildflowers, along with brown mosses and the smooth gray surfaces of rocks protruding through the forest floor. Emily had come to love these colors. The scents were not always pleasant—she happened upon a dead and decaying raccoon on her first day out—and some of the mysterious sounds unnerved her, but the colors were without equal. Mason had told her of how his grandfather made paints and dyes from the plants he collected on the mesa. Each time he pulled up a flower, he thanked it for growing so tall and bright, and he promised to honor it with his creation. Mason shared his grandfather's respect for the land.

"It's peaceful out here," he said. "I'll give it that."

She waited for him to decide. She didn't know what else to do. He would either agree to help her, or he would leave her with the ghost of Sarita and her lover and no way to determine what had happened to them so long ago.

****

Mason drove the bulldozer directly at the man.

"Mace!"

His eyes refocused. He shook off his daydream.

"*Mason!*"

Biting back a curse, Mason stomped down on the clutch with one foot and the brake with the other, bringing the dozer to a shuddering halt just as his friend Jim Hartlet jumped clear.

Hartlet threw off his safety goggles. "Damn, Mason! What the hell are you doing?"

Mason exhaled, his fingers curled around the vehicle's controls. "Sorry, man."

"How could you not see me? Is this neon orange hardhat not bright enough for you?"

He had no excuse. Actually, he *did* have an excuse, that being a green-eyed beauty from the East Coast, but she was no reason to let himself get inattentive at work. His mistake had almost injured a man. "It was an accident," he said. "All I can do is apologize."

"Yeah, okay, it's cool. No harm done. But I think this qualifies me for a smoke break."

"Sure, go ahead."

Hartlet walked off with his chainsaw, digging a pack of cigarettes from his breast pocket.

Mason got back to work. He was clearing deadfall from what would become the path of the truck onto which they'd load the fallen trees. The guys were starting to look at him strangely, as he gave an odd amount of attention to each aspen encountered. What they'd never understand is that helping Emily resolve the shepherd's story had suddenly become more important than his job. He hadn't realized he'd been waiting for something like this until she'd showed him.

He used the broad yellow blade of the bulldozer to drive a pile of woodland debris from his path. The diesel fumes stung his nose. The dozer would probably need servicing soon.

Wait. Was that a carving on a tree?

He put the vehicle in neutral and stood up to get a better look. Sunlight slanted through the trees, forcing him to shield his eyes. But the old, bent aspen was still too far away.

Leaving the dozer idling, he hopped down and jogged to the tree.

Its trunk had been blackened by time, its silvery bark peeling and feathered. Near its base, two parallel gouges were clearly visible. Pulling off his gloves, Mason sank to his knees and touched the rough-edged grooves.

"False alarm," he said softly. Whatever had caused these shallow scratches—an animal or perhaps a hiker—they weren't the work of the anonymous shepherd. The depth of Mason's disappointment surprised him.

Even worse, Emily was only a mile or so away, having a meal with another man.

With a slap of his gloves across his palm, he stood.

Emily was educated, literate, and refined. Under any other circumstances, she never would have crossed paths with Mason Hitapwa, who wore aging cowboy boots and didn't know a salad fork from a dinner fork. He could recite endless verses of Robert Frost, but what was that against a man with a lifetime membership at the Colorado Springs Country Club?

Sometimes, Jimmy White Cloud said, *the sun must move behind the cloud so the people can dance without their shadows.*

Mason went back to the dozer, not wanting to admit that his grandfather was right. He needed to move on and let Emily have her life. With a man like Daggert, she'd want for nothing.

As he threw himself into the bulldozer's seat, Hartlet returned, his goggles riding his forehead. "Hey, Mace. Been meaning to ask, is there something bothering you?"

"Not anymore." He gave the accelerator a push, sending a dragon's breath of black exhaust into the sky.

Chapter Twenty

After sitting down on a fleece blanket that Daggert had produced with the style and flair of a magician, Emily leaned back against a tree and sipped her champagne.

"...and that was the *last* time the city council ever asked me to speak at a monthly meeting, I assure you," he said.

Emily laughed as she'd been laughing most of the day—somewhat artificially, somewhat uncertainly, but for the most part believably.

"You're sure I can't interest you in more pie?"

"I'm fine, Bailey, thank you. And you certainly didn't need to go to so much trouble."

"Not at all. I've had my eye on that bakery ever since it opened a few weeks ago. Glad I had a reason to venture in and sample their wares." He sat with his forearms on his knees, looking confident, if a little out of his element. "I do want to say one thing, and it has nothing to do with apple pie."

Emily didn't know what to expect. "Go ahead."

"I'm not sure if I can help you with the trees. There doesn't seem to be enough rock-hard evidence to support that kind of action. The logging industry doesn't take these things lightly, I promise you, and issuing an order for them to put on the brakes would make the nightly news, to say the least."

"We have a chance to protect a significant piece of regional history."

"I'm sure the significance is open to debate."

"Not to me it isn't."

He let out a breath and tried again. "It's not like we're talking about the great horned owl and its nesting habitat. People can sympathize with that. It's an owl. Owls appear on postage stamps. They're going to have a hard time getting sentimental over some lines on trees."

Emily's cheeks warmed. "Those are not just *lines*."

"You know what I mean."

"A man had a story to tell, a story we will never know if we just…just mow everything down."

"I understand what you're saying, but—"

"You *don't* understand what I'm saying." She returned her empty champagne flute to the basket, using her hands to emphasize her words. "It's not like we're asking to cut off logging permanently and cause some damn paper mill to drop a few points on the stock market. We just want a little time."

"Whose is this *we*? I thought you were in this on your own."

Flustered, Emily waved the question away. She'd unconsciously counted Mason as being on her side, which said more about her feelings for him than she cared to consider at the moment. "The point is that too much of the past is already lost to us. Any little piece we can preserve is important."

"Why?"

"Because those people back then and us—we're the *same*. Their struggles are the same as ours. The only difference is that they didn't live their dramas on social media and reality shows. But the emotions that they felt are no different than the ones we feel today. We're all a part of the same story, so it's our responsibility to protect it." She wasn't sure where any of that had come from or where she was going with it, but she couldn't stop herself.

Just like that night in the Cross Cut, she un-stitched her heart from her sleeve and let it go where it may. "If these were just detached symbols without an obvious human element, like cave drawings of gazelle, then it would be a lot easier for me to step aside. But there was a man here, and he loved a woman with a name. Sarita. And he wanted that love to be recorded so it wouldn't fade away."

"Sarita? How do you know her name?"

"Because he told me. He put a note inside one of the trees." From her bag she produced the photocopy of the shepherd's message, under which she'd written the translation. She handed it to Daggert.

He read it more than once, then looked up. "You found this inside a tree?"

"In a sealed metal tube."

"And you think there could be more out there?"

"I'm an optimist, so yeah, that's what I think. But then again, I also believe we'll achieve lasting world peace one day, so maybe I'm wrong."

Daggert examined the paper again. Emily waited for him to indicate that he was either siding with her or writing her off as a lunatic.

"I trust you won't hold this against me," he finally said, "but my interest in you is more than simply professional."

Emily wouldn't have been surprised if he'd called

her delusional for wanting to hold back the loggers, but this sudden shift completely perplexed her.

"Do you believe that all things happen for a reason?" he asked. "We're out here in the middle of nowhere on a beautiful day, sharing a bubbly and old stories…and I'm going to be bold and say we should gather our rosebuds while we may."

"Rosebuds?" Emily had nothing else to say.

"*Carpe diem*, as the saying goes." He shifted on the blanket. "Come on, Emily, it's not as if I'm asking you to run away to Tahiti. We're two single people enjoying each other's company. That's what days like this were made for."

Emily suddenly thought of several things to say. They all came to her at once. But she pushed them back, hoping to navigate this new minefield in a way that would result in her earning Daggert's agreement without having to sleep with him to get it. Besides, it wasn't as if she'd never before been propositioned on short notice. In her younger days, she'd dallied in one-time trysts more frequently than she cared to recall. But she was a woman now and not a girl, and women had different priorities. Maybe not *higher* priorities, but at least *different*.

"Tell me it doesn't sound fun."

"It's…probably not a good idea."

"To hell with good ideas. It doesn't have to go anywhere after today. If you want us to be two ships in the night, so be it. Such is the richness of life." He touched her leg lightly, invitingly. "But right now…"

She almost pulled away. He had nothing to offer her but a piece of legal paperwork. And all that he asked in return? An hour of emotionless sex.

He moved closer. "You're remarkable. I knew that as soon as we met. I really want to help you, because I think what you've found here is interesting."

"But?"

He smiled, showing teeth as white as those in a mouthwash ad. "*But* maybe it wouldn't hurt to see if we can...work things out between us."

Emily realized what this was: extortion. How had she gotten herself here? Yesterday she was worried about nothing other than saving a few trees and maybe convincing a certain woodcarver that she was worth asking out, but now she was alone with an alpha male who was literally inches away from forcing a sexual favor in exchange for judicial assistance.

Daggert slid his hand a little farther up her leg. His cologne was subtle but distinct. "What do you think? Can we forget about the daily grind for a while and pretend we're silly sixteen-year-olds?"

Overwhelmed, Emily offered no resistance as Daggert drew closer. Just below his left ear was a tiny spot he'd missed when shaving this morning. The little patch of stubble became Emily's focal point as his face hovered over hers.

"Just let it go," he whispered. "Then we'll see if we can work some magic on behalf of dendrogilphs."

Glyphs, she thought fiercely. *They're called dendroglyphs, and they're mine.*

He kissed her forehead.

Suddenly Emily was a decade in her past. Without confidence enough to walk on her own, her crutches waited nearby: a vagabond lover, an unemployment check, the smell of weed in the air. This is how it had been then, when any man with a good body and partial promises could convince her that life was better when lived without responsibility. Things had been uncomplicated back then. She hadn't needed to think for herself. And though she'd left those passive ways behind, it was frightening how easy it would be to tumble back into them, throwing away the woman she'd become.

Daggert put his body against hers and tangled a hand in her hair.

Emily, her back against the tree, instinctively followed his lead, despite the fact that she hadn't let anyone lead her anywhere since she'd remade herself. Daggert guided her down, moving her from the tree and lowering her to the blanket. Like a woman in a coma, she permitted herself to be settled on the ground, this man looming directly above and blocking the sun that sliced through the flickering leaves.

Giving in would take no effort at all. And in the giving, she'd safeguard the shepherd and his beloved. As Daggert eased his weight down on top of her, Emily thought of Sarita. What kind of woman had she been? If she had any sense at all, Sarita just let the world have its way with her and didn't try to struggle. You could find a lot of pleasure in passivity.

Daggert kissed her neck.

Emily closed her eyes.

I wasn't like that at all. These words were not spoken in Magnelli's voice, nor even in Emily's own. They were undeniably feminine.

I am Sarita. I loved a man who drew pictures for me on the trees. And I was strong.

Strong? What use was there for strength when the only way Emily could convince this man to help her

138

was by surrendering? If she couldn't get what she wanted by logical arguments and intelligent reasoning, then she would resort to her old habit: giving up and giving in.

I lived a difficult life in a difficult time. But I found a magnificent power.

So what? Emily arched her neck as Daggert made a necklace of kisses along her throat.

That power was in the man I loved. And that kind of love never backs down.

Daggert's hand, that crafty thing, meandered toward her breasts.

That love made us stronger than the trees themselves. It turned us into gods.

Emily had stopped listening. She had no weapons with which to fight, and so she intended to win by relenting.

The hand slid beneath her shirt.

Pity that you will never know a love like that.

She opened her eyes.

Mason was a storm. His grandfather had told him as much. He was a storm that had blown into her life and made her crave nothing but the touch of his wind and the refreshing laughter of his rain.

Her body stiffened. What had been pliable moments before turned rigid, the muscles tightening in her arms and legs.

Daggert's breath fell on her face. "What's wrong?"

"No more."

He snorted in disbelief, adjusting himself between her legs. "I'm afraid we're past that point." He made a knife blade of his hand and stabbed it down her jeans.

Emily came fully back to herself. She found the

strength that Sarita had known was there all along and gripped Daggert's hair in her fist. *"Get the hell off me."*

His eyes narrowed. "You sure about that?"

"If you don't get up right now, I swear to God I will fight you with everything I have. And I promise, I've got a lot."

His cheeks were flushed with anger and displaced desire. "So much for that injunction you wanted."

"I don't give a damn." She shoved him with both hands."Now get the hell *off!*"

Daggert rolled away from her and scrambled to his feet. His chinos were wrinkled, and the veins stood out in his neck. "This is a stupid move. Do you realize that? Don't say I never offered you a chance."

Emily experienced the somewhat comical urge to give him the finger. She hadn't done that to anyone since junior high. Screw it. She flipped him off.

He grunted. "Yeah. Let's see how far *that* gets you with the loggers." He snatched his phone and keys from the blanket and walked away, leaving everything else behind. "Good luck getting home."

Watching him go, her chest rose and fell as her quickening heart refused to resume a normal rate. She waited for the tears, but they didn't come.

Sarita would have been proud.

Chapter Twenty-One

Mason's phone buzzed once in his pocket.

He planted a boot on a fallen tree, locked down the last chain and waved a signal at the crane operator who would then transfer it to the waiting truck. The crane man gave him the peace sign in reply.

The tree swung ponderously into the air. As he watched it ascend, he slid off his gloves and dug out his phone. Only rarely did anyone get signal here on the mountain. No one bothered to build cell towers in places where bears outnumbered humans.

Removing his sunglasses, he stared at the phone's screen: ONE MISSED CALL.

He pushed a button and saw Emily's name.

Half a minute passed. Mason finally looked up. He'd been thinking about her for the better part of the day, even though he'd already resigned himself to losing her. And seeing her name didn't make it any easier.

He distanced himself from the noisy machinery and dialed his voice mail, but he heard only a beep. Checking the phone, he saw that he had no reception. He stopped and let out a sigh that conveyed everything he felt at the moment. The wisest course of action would be to keep working and worry about the message this evening.

"Sorry, Grandpa," he said. "Your wisdom hasn't

rubbed off quite yet."

He hiked a hundred yards down the track until a single bar appeared on his phone and tried again.

For a moment he heard nothing, and he wondered if she would hang up without saying anything, but then her words came from the silence: "Mason, hey, it's me. I, uh, I'm sort of stuck out here. This whole thing didn't go very well. Daggert is…he's gone. The bastard tried to force himself on me, and I don't have a way back to the motel. I was…wondering if you could come."

Then the automated voice said, "End of new messages."

Mason stared at the phone as if he'd misheard. *The bastard tried to force himself on me.*

He turned and ran for the nearest truck.

****

Emily walked through the woods, following the trail that would eventually lead back to Rockerton. The day was warm, but she couldn't shake a chill. Every few minutes she gave both arms a vigorous rub.

Daggert by now was halfway back to Colorado Springs, taking his injunction with him. Emily hoped she'd never see the man again. Of course, her actions had their consequences. Unless she could find another willing judge within the next twenty-four hours, the remainder of the trees near the shepherd's stomping ground would be bound for the mill.

Would Magnelli help further? She dreaded having to call and ask.

She turned and looked back. The sound of the trucks and saws carried down the slope.

She resumed her march. More than anything, she was angry at herself. Had she said or done something to make Daggert think she was interested? Yeah, probably so. She'd flirted with him, if only a little, thinking she could charm him into getting what she wanted. Maybe she'd led him on, so she had only herself to blame for getting groped. And now she was alone in a forest with a phone with spotty service. When she'd conceived the idea for her dissertation, this was certainly *not* the way she'd envisioned it working out.

A horn blasted behind her.

She immediately dashed to the side. After such a crappy day, getting run over by a logging truck wouldn't have surprised her, but as she turned to get a look at it, she saw Mason behind the wheel. She let out a little sound of relief.

He'd no sooner hit the brakes and opened his door than she ran to him and—before he could say anything—she threw her arms around his neck.

He hugged her back. "Hey, it's okay…"

She said nothing, just closed her eyes and gripped him tighter.

After a few seconds, he stepped back and held her at arm's length. "Is Daggert gone?"

She nodded.

"Did he…hurt you?"

She shook her head.

"Say something, Em."

She gave him the best smile she could. "I'm so glad to see you."

"And I'm glad to hear you say that."

If Emily had entertained any doubts about how Mason felt for her, they turned to mist and drifted through the forest canopy. His eyes told her everything she needed to know. She'd never considered herself the

most intuitive of women or the best judge of men—
Daggert had certainly made *that* one clear—but she
trusted what she saw in Mason's face.

"Care to give a girl a lift?"

"They say never to pick up hitchhikers."

"Even especially desperate ones?"

"Those are probably the worst kind."

"I can be very convincing."

One brow arched toward his hairline. "Oh, yeah?"

"For example, I can offer to buy dinner."

"Maybe I've already eaten."

"I can pay for gas."

"It's not my truck."

"How about if I punch you in the nose if you don't
shut up and say yes?"

He laughed. "You talked me into it."

"I can be very persuasive when I want to."

"No doubt about it." As they walked together
toward the pickup, he said, "Are you sure you're
okay?"

"It's my own fault for not seeing what a jerk he is."

"You had no way of knowing."

"Maybe I was just so intent on the task at hand that
I turned a blind eye to his general assholiness."

"Assholiness? Is that even a word?"

"If the shoe fits."

"Yeah. So…I guess that means he won't be helping
us out."

"I don't want to talk about it anymore."

"But if we can't keep them from—"

"*Dinner*. That's what I want to talk about. I'm in
the mood for fried rice. Is there a Chinese place in
town? I like the ones where they give you the take-out

in those little cardboard pagodas."

He looked at her askance. "You're impossible."

"No. I'm just bantering to keep from crying. Can't you tell?"

She got in and slammed the door, embarrassed that she'd let Daggert take advantage of her. But Mason was here now, sliding behind the wheel only two feet away from her. Why did that make everything better? She hadn't known him for very long at all, and yet...

"Pagodas, huh?" he asked as he got them moving.

"And wine. Pagodas and wine."

"Sounds like a dangerous combination."

She watched him in profile as he drove. *So do we.*

Chapter Twenty-Two

Mason had built the coffee table that was now laden with the remains of Chinese take-out, a half-empty bottle of plum wine, two wine glasses, and four chopsticks that had quickly been abandoned in favor of the less elegant but far more practical forks.

"Is there anything in this house you *didn't* make yourself?" she asked.

Mason bunched his eyebrows dramatically as he considered it. He was simply having fun, and so he felt like goofing around. Maybe it was the wine loosening his knots or maybe he was just happy to be enjoying himself. Either way, he liked acting silly with her, if only to hear her laugh. That was the one thing his house lacked more than any other: laughter.

"Well?"

"Um, I didn't build this couch we're sitting on."

"You don't do couches?"

"I guess I never tried."

"But the kitchen table?"

He nodded.

"And these picture frames?"

"A few of them."

"That's an awful lot of work."

"Some guys surf the internet. Some fish."

"And you make baby bassinets."

"As long as someone's willing to pay for it." The

last two hours had been his favorites. Not just his favorites of the day, but possibly the month. Hell, it was longer than a month. No use lying to himself. His days had been mundane until almost running this woman over. "If people would start having more babies, maybe I could quit my day job."

Emily lifted her wine glass and made a point of inspecting its contents. "I want you to know that I'm a lousy drunk, so I'm stopping after these final two swallows."

"I'll make sure to hide your car keys, just in case."

She smiled. "You know, car ownership is one more thing you and I have in common."

"What do you mean?"

"You drive company vehicles, right? Well, I don't own a car, either."

"Public transit?"

"Every chance I get. I live about three blocks from campus, so I walk when the weather's nice. But the bus runs right in front of my apartment, so I'm okay on the lousy days, too. And we have a lot of those. It's a little inconvenient, sometimes, having to hitch a ride with a girlfriend when the bus isn't running where I need to go, but I sold my old heap when I entered the Ph.D. program and promised myself I wasn't buying anything new until after I graduated."

"Rewarding yourself, huh?"

"If I ever manage to get my dissertation written and defended, yes. But what about you? There aren't a lot of busses running up the side of the mountain. If you quit your day job and go woodworker full time, you'll need to invest some of that bassinet money in a Jeep."

"A Jeep? Maybe. I like them with the tops off in

the summer. But, uh, I guess driving a car of my own is…something I need to deal with."

Emily tilted her head to the side. "You lost me on that one."

At that moment, Mason realized that maybe these two hours weren't his favorites, after all. They'd brought him to this place he tried to avoid. How had he not seen this coming and guided the conversation elsewhere?

"Mason?"

He looked at his wine glass but fought off the urge to return to the bottle. Medication by way of alcohol hadn't worked after the accident—though damned if he hadn't tried—and it wouldn't work now. "My car was totaled when I hit a delivery van on Highway 160 at twenty minutes past eleven on a Wednesday night."

Emily put a hand over her mouth.

Mason hated this. He hated giving voice to those events again because those people were wrong when they said that time healed all wounds. "I remember the time exactly because when I opened my eyes, I was upside-down, and…" He swallowed. "And I saw a watch in front of my face. Its glass was cracked. It was stopped at eleven-twenty."

He waited for Emily to say what everybody said: *Oh, my god. Were you hurt? That's horrible. Was the other driver okay?*

But again she surprised him. She put her glass on the table, visibly gathered herself, and looked at him with gentle understanding. "The woman in the photograph was with you."

Mason automatically looked in the direction of the picture on the fridge, though the kitchen had been claimed by shadows and revealed little to him. "How did you know?"

Emily rested her hand lightly on his knee. "What was her name?"

The heavy beat in his heart made him want to get up from this couch and run. This is not how he'd intended things to unfold tonight. He wanted this woman's friendship and possibly her affection, but he didn't need her sympathy.

She squeezed his leg. "Don't answer that. It's none of my business and—"

"Brianna. Her name was Brianna Hitapwa."

"That's...a beautiful name."

"She was my sister."

Emily lowered her eyes. Mason was thankful, because he felt his own welling up, just as they had done so often. "The watch I saw in front of my face that night was hers. We'd been fighting. We were adults, but sometimes we fought like I was still twelve and she was still ten. Just two kids, you know. I turned to say something to her. I looked away from the road for only a second. A *second*." He blinked and managed to hold the tears at the rim of his eyes, though he knew that if he went on much longer, they'd tumble down his face. "Anyway, I haven't owned a car since then. Excuse me." He got up, steadied himself, and turned toward the bathroom.

"I'm so sorry. I had no idea."

He nodded his thanks but said nothing. The bathroom offered him what Brianna used to call a Primping Pit Stop. Just a few seconds to check herself in the mirror, adjust her hair...Mason used his own version of the Pit Stop to lean over the toilet and wait for either his stomach to settle or his fried rice to make a return trip.

A minute later, Emily knocked softly at the door. "I'm not going anywhere."

He wiped a line of sweat from his upper lip. He didn't usually react like this when thinking of his little sister. But the confluence of emotions was too taxing. His feelings for Emily seemed to be evolving by the hour, and combined with his grief for Brianna, it was too much to handle without being sick.

"Did you hear me? I'll sit out here all night by this door if I have to."

"I'm fine," he said.

"You're a liar."

"Excuse me?"

"You're not fine at all. And you're not *supposed* to be. I don't know anything at all about the accident, and I never knew your sister. But I know *you*. At least, I think I do. And it's okay for you to feel like the world is ending and it's okay to hide in the bathroom. It's also okay for me to stay here and wait for you to come out."

Mason's admiration for her only grew. He wanted to hurl open the door and pull her into his arms, but then he would break down completely. If he ever got lucky enough to hold her, he didn't want to be crying when he did.

"Take your time," Emily said. "I'm planting my butt on your floor."

Mason looked at himself in the mirror. Maybe he could use a little Primping Pit Stop, after all. He wiped his eyes. Blew his nose. Ran a hand through his hair.

Then he opened the door.

Emily sat on the hardwood floor just outside the

bathroom, legs crossed, back against the wall. "And here I was bracing myself to sit till dawn."

He squatted beside her, balancing on the balls of his feet. "You're right. I'm a liar."

"Everybody gets a few lies to use without penalty. Yours went to a good cause."

"You're incredible, you know that?"

She smiled in a way that made her green eyes glitter. "No, I don't know. Say it again to convince me."

"You are incredible."

"Again."

"Don't push your luck."

She laughed. Mason helped her to her feet, suggested a walk outside, and as they stepped out under the Colorado sky, he asked himself if he was falling for her.

If the answer was yes, then how hard and how far?

"This is why I bought the tent," Emily said, looking up at the stars. "When I was planning this trip, I could have opted to get a motel room every night. But then I wouldn't have been able to see *that* every night." She swept her arm upward, encompassing all the heavens. "It's a lot different view from the city."

"I've never been," he admitted.

"To New Jersey?"

"To a city."

"You've never been to a city?"

"Does Colorado Springs count?"

She stopped and looked at him. "You're kidding."

He enjoyed watching her face in the starlight, the shadows on her cheeks. "I've driven through a few on the interstate. I've stopped for gas here and there. But I rarely hang around."

"Too crowded?"

"It's not that. Blame it on the red man in me."

"So now you're stereotyping yourself?"

"Sometimes the stereotypes are true. Indians and rush-hour traffic don't mix."

"That idea is a little dated, isn't it?"

He chuckled. "I really wish you could've met my grandfather. You don't know the meaning of the term *old school* until you've spent some time on the back of a mule with Jimmy White Cloud Hitapwa."

"If he's half as incorrigible as his grandson, I'm sure it would've been an interesting experience. As for the idea of riding a mule…"

"Ah, we're even."

"Even?"

"I've never been to a big city, and you've never ridden a mule."

"You've got me on that one."

"Or squeezed venom from a rattlesnake's fangs."

"Okay, you've got me on that one, too."

"Or smoked peyote at an ancestor dance."

She poked him in the arm. "All right, you've made your point. I'm a stiff and boring city-dweller, not to mention hopelessly uncultured."

"I wouldn't say hopelessly. Maybe I can find a rattlesnake out here and let you practice milking its venom."

"Uh, that ancestor dance sounds a bit more to my liking, if you don't mind."

"You have a bias against snake-handlers?"

"I think that's a bit *too* much culture, thank you."

Laughing was so easy with her. He didn't want these stars to go away. If they would only linger, maybe he and Emily could stay out here forever, talking like old friends. Thoughts of Brianna eased away, releasing the pressure from his chest. Underneath the current of Emily's words, didn't he detect something else? Or was he alone in his anticipation?

But then Emily darkened. "How long before the loggers arrive?"

He didn't want to talk about it, but now that she'd taken such a rapid turn, he supposed he had no choice but to follow. "We're scheduled to get to the edge of your campsite by late afternoon tomorrow."

She looked down.

"I can stall them," Mason offered, as panic encroached. He refused to lose her over this. "The foreman put me in charge of this part of the crew. I can delay them."

"How?"

"The company really stresses safety. We haven't had a full drill in about three weeks. I can call for a full inspection and maintenance of all the equipment, and that'll eat up at least two hours. That would mean you'd have until the next morning, the day after tomorrow. But that's all I can do."

"And that's it? That's all we've got?"

"You'll have to move fast."

"There are too many trees."

"I know."

"And we haven't even found the cave."

"Short of sabotaging the operation, that's all I can do. I've killed myself trying to come up with a miracle, but I don't have any. Maybe Jimmy White Cloud could've conjured a summer snowstorm and shut everything down, but I don't have his magic. God knows I wish I did."

She nodded, still not looking at him, hands thrust into the back pockets of her jeans.

This wasn't the way to her heart. If he had any hope of winning her—and that hope was becoming more pronounced the longer he was around her—then he had to find a way to bring her this thing she wanted most of all. To hand her the full story of Sarita and the shepherd was noble and romantic and all of that, but it was also apparently impossible.

"I should go," Emily said. "I'll need to get an early start in the morning."

Mason didn't want her to leave. Just looking at her standing there made him think of things he hadn't considered in years. When was the last time he'd met a woman like this?

Never. He reached for her. "Hey…"

"I know, you're sorry it has to be this way. I'll just have to…to be really quick tomorrow and take lots of pictures. It's not like those trees were going to last forever, anyway. There's a chance I might miss something if I hurry, but I'll get high on coffee beforehand so my radar stays nice and perky…"

He withdrew his hand. He simply wanted to touch her, as if to hold her to this spot and not let her fly away when her work here was over. But she was not the kind to be restrained, and that made her all the more alluring. "I'll get the truck keys."

They returned to the house. Mason wanted to ask her to stay for a while longer and he wanted to defend her trees and he wanted to tell her all about Brianna. But he put his wants away, knowing they'd come back to haunt him when she was gone.

****

Emily didn't want to leave.

Standing on his porch in a sweater she hadn't worn since last autumn, she weighed her options, each one more outlandish than the last. Stay and talk to this man all night. Steal away into the dark forest with him and try to find the trees by touch. Take his hand and put a single kiss in the center of his palm, just to see where it would lead.

Shake it off, old girl, Magnelli warned. *Many a researcher has been lost forever to such flights of foolish fancy.*

Right. Focus on the work to be accomplished in the morning. She needed to get to bed and sleep soundly so as to have energy for tomorrow's frantic search. As the loggers closed in, Emily would skip from one aspen to the next, looking for the shepherd's elusive signs. She couldn't worry about anything else, especially unproductive romantic urges.

"Ready?" Mason asked, spinning the keys on his finger.

"As I'll ever be."

They went to the truck. He held her door for her.

When they were moving, driving through the yellow tunnel created by the headlights, Mason said, "I'm serious about calling for that inspection. If I do things by the book, a drill like that could easily burn off a couple of hours. The guys don't mind, because it gives them a break from the routine. I know it's not much, but that's all the time I can buy you."

"I appreciate it. Really. I'll do what I can."

"I'm sorry it has to happen like this."

"Stop saying that."

"Can't. I'm the guy who's about to level your life's work."

"First of all, you're doing it because you have to, not because you're vindictive. And secondly, this is hardly my life's work. There are at least twenty-nine thousand other topics I can choose for my dissertation."

"Maybe, but I'm also sorry for *him*."

"Him who?"

"Sarita's boyfriend. I'm really starting to relate to him. I know it sounds crazy but...can't you just imagine him alone up here with his sheep, before most of these trees were even standing? He was up here working, sure, but I don't think his mind was entirely on his flock."

"To be sure."

"And I think that's cool. I mean, a hundred years ago, that could've been me."

"Well, if it *was* you, then I'd wish that you'd please recall your past life so that you can tell me just where that stupid cave happens to be and what the hell's in it."

He thought about it for a few silent moments. "Maybe I'll dream the answer for you tonight."

"I'd appreciate that. Personally I don't think I'll be able to sleep at all."

"I suppose you could be like the shepherd and count sheep."

She rolled her eyes. "Funny man."

"Maybe in a past life I was also a comedian."

"Judging by that joke, I wouldn't count on it."

"Hey!"

She enjoyed the remainder of the ride, teasing him, being teased by him, and delighting in the flirting that had suddenly turned overt. There was no more hiding it.

She got out of the truck in front of her motel room. "I'll be okay tomorrow," she assured him before he could ask. "Just do your thing and I'll do mine."

He paused for only a second before saying, "I want our things to be the same."

Emily looked at him through the open door, searching for an appropriate response.

"Goodnight, Emily." He leaned across the seat, tugged the door shut, and drove away.

She crossed her arms and watched him until his taillights faded from sight.

What had he just said?

"I want our things to be the same," she echoed, then turned and walked slowly toward her room, wondering.

Chapter Twenty-Three

She awoke before dawn and had Tunny stop at a convenience store so she could fill her insulated mug with mediocre coffee. Her prediction about sleep had been partially correct. She'd slept in starts and stops, like a car inching its way through city traffic. She counted on the caffeine and a general sense of urgency to fuel her these first few hours of the new day.

By the time she waved goodbye to Tunny and approached her base camp, the sun had turned the eastern sky from black to an optimistic orange. Wandering lightning bugs flickered their lanterns between the trees.

She opened her field book and scanned the grid she'd drawn. This was it. She had no more time for methodic work, no more time for drawing obsessive-compulsive diagrams on paper and connecting the dots. Very soon the din of chainsaws would commence, and by and by she'd catch glimpses of men approaching through the trees. Maybe Mason could slow them down and maybe he couldn't. Either way, she would depend only on herself.

With her gear-filled bag over her shoulder, she struck out through the woods.

Signs of her previous excursions were evident in the tamped-down grass and broken twigs. She hadn't come here as a gentle visitor who left no trace but rather as an interloper in someone else's story. She concentrated on her steps, always mindful of twisting an ankle, but it was only a minute or so before she heard Mason's voice in her head again, the very voice that had kept her up a good portion of the night. There had been a point at about four in the morning when Emily had wished that he wasn't such a gentleman. Had he a bit of the kidnapper in him and attempted to hold her hostage at his cabin, she would not have given him much resistance.

"There, I admit it," she said to the trees. "Now stop pestering me about it."

The trees, in their wisdom, offered no reply.

How long had it been since she'd had a lover? Never mind the men who never advanced beyond the boyfriend stage, and forget everything that had happened while Emily was drifting through her pre-college days. Counting only the last eight years or so and *not* counting the casual dates, please, Ms. Radsco, tell the jury just *how long*.

"You don't want to know."

She went from tree to tree as she always did, but this time didn't stop to record the precise coordinates of each one. Instead, she simply drew a quick squiggle on her grid and moved to the next.

Eight squiggles later, she found a dendroglyph.

The sight of it shocked her. She hadn't really been expecting to find anything. Yet it was there, dark against the pale silver bark, almost like a wood burn. She fell to her knees in the dew and ran her hands along the surface of it.

The cave was again represented, a circle open at one end. This time, however, two figures were depicted *inside* the cave—the man and the woman. Between them was an oblong shape that Emily couldn't identify. It was so faded that it might have simply been a random slash on the bark.

"They're together," Emily said. She jerked the bag from her shoulder and plumbed its depths until she located her phone. Then she took twenty pictures from different angles, turning the flash on and off in order to ensure that she ended up with workable results. That done, she put a piece of rice paper against the image and made a rubbing, though it didn't turn out as precise as she would have liked.

Had Sarita and her lover ended up with each other? Or was this just the shepherd doing a bit of understandable wishful thinking?

Emily had to know.

Hastily noting the GPS position of the tree, she went to the next and proceeded from there. She worked for two hours and stopped only once to look in the direction of the now very audible saws and heavy trucks. She couldn't see them through the many layers of trees, but they couldn't have been more than a hundred yards away, maybe even as close as fifty.

Lunch consisted of a Washington apple eaten on the move, followed by a protein bar that tasted suspiciously like crumbled cardboard. This was no way to perform academic research. She'd given up on methodology and was now just a woman with apple juice running down her chin, jogging between the trees.

At a little past one in the afternoon, she saw a bullet hole.

Except this wasn't a bullet hole at all. This was the butt end of another small tube the shepherd had hammered like a nail into the tree.

"Hello, gorgeous."

It was a miracle that she'd even seen it. The circle was darker than the wood around it, but it wasn't large or especially prominent. She dug her fingers into the shallow pore the thing had made in the bark. But like the previous capsule they'd discovered, it was too deep and too overgrown to remove without tools.

"Dammit!" Emily struck it with the edge of her hand. She carried a small pocketknife in her bag, but its two-inch blade wouldn't get her very far.

Now what?

She had nothing else that might work. Looking around was pointless, but she did so automatically, as if she might find a chisel and hammer lying among the toadstools. Her pulse picked up considerably as the excitement of the find coursed through her, and she was eager to dig out the shepherd's latest treasure—but how?

"Mason."

She needed to tell him, to share it with him, to make him a part of it. And, incidentally, she also needed his tools. She dropped her bag at the tree's base and pressed a button on her GPS device that marked her present location. Then she turned and made her way through the forest, heading toward the sound of buzzing saws.

****

"Radio check," Mason said.

"Which frequency?" Hartlet asked.

"Non-emergency. You guys have been checking your batteries, right?"

"More or less."

"Phones are unreliable out here," Mason reminded the half-dozen men gathered around him. "We depend on these walkie-talkies, so it's important that you replace the batteries every few months. Got it?"

"Sure," Hartlet said. "Why all the sudden worry?"

"I'm not worried. Just being careful."

"Mace, I've worked with you for four years now, and you've been crew chief for half that time, and I ain't *never* heard you going on about checking our batteries."

"Maybe he's gunnin' for a promotion," Luiz suggested with a grin.

"Nah, it's something else." Hartlet cocked his thumbs into his leather work belt. "You doing okay, Mace? You been acting kind of funny lately."

Mason looked at their dirty, bearded faces. Three of them were white, two were black, and one—Luiz—was a wiry Latino who was quick to laugh. Mason was the only Indian among them, and never once had he ever felt as if they understood what he was about. Had they traveled the same roads, read the same poems, suffered the same loss? "Just humor me, guys. The boss says we need to check the radios occasionally, so what are we going to do?"

"Check the radios," they muttered.

"Then let's get to it."

The men pawed the units from their belts, knocked the sawdust from them, and spent a few minutes ensuring that everything was functioning as intended.

"If anyone is still using the older model," Mason said, "we're supposed to get some more upgrades in a month or so."

"We won't hold our breath," Hartlet said.

"Hey, you never know. We might get lucky. Anyway, the older ones aren't exactly as water-resistant as they should be, so we're going to need to—"

"Uh, Mace?"

"What is it?"

"There's somebody comin' through the woods."

Everyone turned. They saw a flash of color moving between the trees.

"Looks like a *woman*," Hartlet said.

"Emily." Mason had been spending the day trying to think of anything but this woman who had captivated him, but now here she was, appearing like a figure in a dream. "Emily?"

"You know her?"

He ran toward her, leaving the men to stare after him with puzzled looks on their faces.

"Mason!" They converged and held each other's arms. "*I found one.*"

"Another symbol?"

"A message, a note…it's stuck in the tree just like the other one."

"One of the cylinders?"

She nodded, breathing heavily from the exertion of her trip.

"Did you get it out?"

"Couldn't. It's stuck. I need you."

"You've got me. I'll grab my gear." He left her only long enough to retrieve a few tools, then the two of them set off, holding hands as they went.

"Hey, Mace!" Luiz yelled.

Mason turned but kept moving. "Yeah?"

"What's going on?"

"I'll tell you later," he replied, knowing that he

never would.

Chapter Twenty-Four

With Mason's hand in hers, Emily retraced her steps, following the path the GPS set before her.

"You're sure that's what it was?" he asked. "It wasn't just a knothole or something?"

"You think I imagined it?"

"Just asking."

"I know what I saw. Sorry to interrupt you at work, by the way."

"I've been waiting to be interrupted all day. What took you so long?"

"Your friends probably think you're insane, tromping off into the woods with a random woman."

"You're not so random."

"Feels that way sometimes."

They walked without speaking for a few minutes, weaving through the trees. Then Mason squeezed her hand, and she looked over at him.

"This is cool as hell," he said.

Emily smiled. She hadn't held hands with a man in…had it been that long? Walking through the forest with him was a simple delight, even though they were moving double-time and ducking under low-hanging branches instead of enjoying a leisurely stroll. "What are they going to say to when you go back?"

"Who said I was going back?"

"I won't be responsible for your unemployment."

"Maybe this is the incentive I need."

"Incentive for what?"

"Selling my carpentry designs. Getting my stuff into the stores in Denver and Boulder. Taking a chance and doing what I love."

"I don't think the path of the starving artist is all it's cracked up to be."

"You're saying I shouldn't try it?"

"I think your work is beautiful. And you'll probably end up earning more from it than I ever will by teaching survey anthropology courses. But quitting your day job—"

"Is risky."

"Yeah."

"But worth it. I think the shepherd would agree with me."

Emily liked the idea of Mason comparing himself to the shepherd, if only because she'd done the same thing with Sarita. What would it have been like to be a girl in the barely tamed west of Colorado, in a time when horse-drawn wagons were still more commonplace than cars? Leaning on her windowsill and staring up at the distant mountain, Sarita daydreamed of a young man who guarded his flock from wolves while thinking about her. Perhaps their parents didn't approve, and so the two of them had sought out a cave…

"I think you're right," she said. "He *would* agree."

They reached the tree.

"There." She crouched. "Do you see it? That's no knothole."

"Definitely not." He broke out his tools and began tapping, sawing, and prying.

Emily tried to be patient but had little luck. She could do nothing but watch him work, and so she did, realizing that this was something of a pleasant pastime. He wore a short-sleeved T-shirt that was pulled taut across his shoulders as he bent over. His arms were naturally the color of bronze. His hair was as black as any Emily had seen, and she smiled at herself when she felt a physical urge to pass her fingers through it.

"This is in deeper than the last one," Mason said. "Another year or so, and the tree would've probably sealed it up completely."

"Maybe not. This tree is mostly dead, I think. It's over a hundred years old, poor thing."

"Happens to all of us. The spirit of this tree has business elsewhere. It did what it came here to do."

"And what did it come here to do?"

"Give life and shade to the forest. Provide a home for birds and a place for caterpillars to turn into butterflies. If this tree hadn't been here, generations of those animals and insects never would have happened."

Emily loved it when he philosophized like this. It made her understand that the universe was bigger than she imagined. Everything was connected. "I also found another carving, by the way."

He looked up briefly. "What was it?"

"The cave. With two people inside."

"No kidding?" He attacked the buried cylinder with even greater enthusiasm.

"We need to find that place."

"It could be buried under tons of rock by now. An avalanche, earth tremor, natural erosion—a lot could've happened to it in the last century."

"Maybe there's a map to it in that cylinder."

"Yeah, you think this shepherd could make things a little easier on us." Mason leaned into his screwdriver, which performed as a pry bar, slowly inching the rusty metal tube from the wood. Then he switched to a pair of locking pliers, clamped them down, and braced his feet against the tree. "This is the part where I throw my back out of alignment."

He pulled.

The object slid out so suddenly that Mason fell backward. Emily helped him up, and he unlocked the pliers, letting the cylinder drop into her hand.

"Do we need to go back to your house to cut it open?" she asked.

"Not this time. I have a hacksaw."

"You do? Well, I knew I brought you along for *some* reason."

He winked at her and put his saw in motion. With the tube braced against a flat stone, he gently drew and pushed the blade, which cut through the crumbling metal with the efficiency of a laser. "Hold out your hands."

Kneeling beside him, Emily did so, cupping the tightly rolled paper as it slid free. "Now the trick is getting it open without ripping it." Keeping her touch as light as possible, she pinched the corner and slowly unwound it.

Mason seemed equally enthralled. He leaned so close that his breath fell on her fingers as she peeled back the paper. "I think I see something."

Emily saw it, too. The words were terribly faint. Whatever ink the shepherd had used had long ago lost most of its substance. If not for its container, it surely would have faded completely. "We're not going to be able to read it, not unless you brought a satellite phone with a Spanish-English dictionary app along with your hacksaw."

"Sorry, my foresight goes only so far."

"You're forgiven." She nudged the note open a little more. "There's a field book in my bag. Can you get it?"

He found her notebook.

"Write this down." Holding the delicate page close to her eyes, she read the Spanish aloud, spelling each individual word.

"Something about the evening?" Mason ventured.

"Or night-time," Emily said. "That's the only word that looks familiar. But keep in mind that our shepherd isn't a spelling-bee champion, so there may be other words in here that we might otherwise recognize."

Mason's free-flowing penmanship glided under the notes she'd made in her exact handwriting, like a cloud passing under a perfect sky. "Got it," he said.

Emily returned the note to its original state but didn't try to replace it in the cylinder for fear of damaging it. "I need to get online and translate this."

"*We*."

She smiled at him. "You're right. *We*. Sorry."

He poked her playfully on the elbow. "Don't let it happen again."

She held up three fingers. "Girl Scout's honor."

"I'll drive," he said.

"And they'll be okay with that? You can just leave in the middle of the day?"

"You know what? I don't think I care anymore what they think or whether or not it's okay."

"Again, I don't want to be responsible for your

getting fired."

"Maybe getting fired would be for the best."

Emily put her bag over her shoulder and laced her fingers in his. There was something very basic about holding hands. It didn't matter if you were twelve or eighty-two; holding hands with someone never got old.

"You want the bad news?" Mason asked as they moved between the trees.

"Not especially."

"Even if I leave the job early today, they're going to keep working, keep cutting. I bought us a few hours, and there's not much time left in the work day, but they'll be at your camp by ten in the morning at the latest."

Emily tried not to think about that. She concentrated on the feeling of his hand. For now, that was enough.

Chapter Twenty-Five

In Mason's cabin, with a mug of black coffee in hand, Emily stood over his shoulder as he entered the Spanish-language text into the online translator.

"You should be doing the typing here," he said. "I don't exactly do a hundred words a minute."

"You hunt and peck with the best of them."

"Sure, as I long as I'm watching my hands."

She gave him an encouraging squeeze on the shoulder but made sure not to let her hand linger, as much as she wanted to. The longer she stood in his domain, surrounded by his scent and his finely wrought wooden things, the more difficult it was to fight this new and possibly reckless desire.

"Okay, let's see what we have." He clicked the icon marked TRANSLATE.

Emily leaned over him and read, automatically correcting for the oddities of the interpreter. "'When the moon next rises, I will see you where the hill teeth smile. Wait for me if I am late, my Sarita.'"

"Hill teeth?" Mason asked. "That can't be right."

"What was the word the shepherd used?"

Mason checked the notes. "*Dientes.*"

"What's the dictionary say?"

Mason switched web pages and entered the term in the dictionary. "Nope, that's right. Teeth. Is there anywhere with that name on your maps?"

"You're not familiar with it?"

"Never heard of it."

"Then we'll have to assume that the name's changed over time."

"Or he's speaking in metaphor."

"If he's speaking in metaphor then we may *never* figure out what he's talking about."

"We have to," Mason said.

"But what if we don't? What if we can't?" A sudden pessimist appeared in her head, fearful that they'd never locate the shepherd's rendezvous place, fearful that the loggers would take it away, fearful that the sky was falling. "Maybe it's time we prepared ourselves for the very real possibility that none of this is going to work out the way we want."

"I can't do that."

"You're going to magically make it turn out okay?"

"If I have to, yes. Maybe I'll find some of that medicine that my grandfather had and call upon the spirits of my ancestors to show us the way."

"I wish it were that easy…"

"*It is.*" Mason spun in the office chair so that he faced her, then tugged her hand.

At his bidding, she dropped into a crouch in front of him.

Mason carefully picked up the shepherd's rolled note, placed it on Emily's palm, and held her fingers. "Okay, here it goes."

"Here goes what?"

"Maybe you don't realize how important this is."

She stared into his earth-brown eyes and couldn't look away.

He seemed to be gathering his thoughts. The longer he sat there, touching her, the more trouble Emily had with her heart: it kept beating faster.

"This has nothing to do with preserving history," he finally said. "At least not for me. This is more than that. This is their lives coming back to us, their love affair making itself known after all this time, probably the most spectacular thing that ever happened to them, and now it's back. It's like…their echo. And we're holding it here in our hands."

Emily breathed very slowly, her chest rising and falling, rising and falling.

"I don't know anything about him," Mason went on. "This shepherd—he's a total enigma to me. Except for one thing. He fell in love with a woman, and when he should've been working, he was busy tapping notes into aspen trees. I…I can identify with that."

Emily closed her eyes, letting that move through her.

"Hey."

She opened her eyes.

"I don't know where you and I are going, and maybe it won't even last past tomorrow when the crew harvests the last of the trees, but right now, right here in my own house, I'm no different than that shepherd. I'm just a guy hoping a girl will meet me at the cave."

When Emily moved, she did so like a woman under the sea. The very air seemed to press in all around her, so that when she reached to put the rolled note on the desk, she did it like she was submerged. Without a sound she touched his hair and deliberately moved her fingers through it. Her own need surprised her with its intensity. She'd gone for so long giving all of her energy to intellectual pursuits that this physical yearning was almost foreign to her—foreign and familiar at the same time.

"Am I just embarrassing myself here?" he wondered aloud.

Emily gave him the slightest smile in her arsenal, one that said everything telepathically: *No, there is no embarrassment here, only a sweet understanding...*

From his hair she let her fingers roam his face. As if she were blind and knowing him by touch, she traveled his cheeks and chin, her fingertips tingling in anticipation. Mason, captive to her touch, could only sit there and let her explore him. The hand that had so recently felt for dendroglyphs now explored his face.

"You are the storm," Emily said softly, recalling the words of Mason's grandfather. "I needed help to drive away those who would harm the shepherd's aspens, and Sky Father sent you to me."

Mason nodded almost imperceptibly.

Emily drew her finger down his neck and found his chest. She roamed his neckline, then went down from there. His pectorals were firm beneath her touch. She wanted to memorize him. She wanted to hold his shape in her mind so that she would never forget this moment when he'd told her of the echo and invited her to relive it with him. Had Sarita known a time like this? When she was first alone with the shepherd, had she yearned to tumble into him, to lose her own identity for a while?

She sent her finger lower.

Mason grabbed her hand and stopped her. Without taking his eyes from hers, he lifted her palm and kissed the center of it, where seconds before the shepherd's note had rested. From that kiss, Emily imagined she could feel its impact moving up her arm. She needed more of that, needed it in a way that rapidly dissolved her ability to think.

Mason took her hand and placed it on his own shoulder. He found her other hand and did the same. Then he took her face in his hands, leaned forward, and kissed her lightly. It was the kind of kiss that was exploratory and hinted of things to come. His lips were warm.

Overcome, Emily embraced him around the neck and crushed her mouth against his.

The kiss went on. Emily didn't want it to end, but she had to withdraw simply to catch her breath. Mason captured her before she could pull away. He stood, guiding her up with him. He kissed her again, deeply and completely, and she rose on her toes to meet him.

She wanted his hands on her, but for now he kept them lightly on her arms, as if all his thoughts were funneled into that kiss. His mouth was warm, and when the tip of his tongue touched hers, she made a noise to let him know that she shared his craving.

He turned her as if they were dancers. Then he stepped toward her, bumping her into the desk. She widened her stance, inviting him to move even closer. He edged between her legs.

Emily let herself go. It had been too long since she'd fallen with such abandon. But as Mason placed his hands tenderly against her back, she knew that this was different. This was not a man who simply wanted to take something from her, to satisfy his own hunger. He wanted the two of them to honor Sarita and her lover, to continue the story that they'd been given.

He took his hands away suddenly, causing Emily to

gasp. He pulled his shirt over his head, dropped it, and kissed her again.

Emily's hands explored his body, the smooth plane of his back, the slope of his shoulders, the hardness of his chest. His heat amazed her, and she wanted it against her. She raised her arms toward the ceiling, and as if reading her mind, took her shirt and let her hair spill through as he lifted it up and away. When they resumed their embrace, the feeling of his skin thrilled her.

If Mason seemed at times quiet and reserved, he displayed none of that as he deftly released her bra and kissed down the length of her neck as he removed it. Emily tangled her fingers in his hair and pushed herself against him, using the desk behind her for leverage. Mason responded, leaning harder into her, his hands writing their own kind of inscriptions on her back.

She leaned back, arching her neck, her hair hanging down as he kissed between her breasts and then down her stomach. She didn't let go of his hair— she *couldn't*—as he unfastened her pants and glided them down her legs. She stepped out of them, and then her panties, wanting him to hurry, dammit, just hurry so that she could get as much of her bare skin touching his as possible.

He lifted her easily and sat her on the desk. His pushed his jeans down, and then she wrapped her legs around him and locked her ankles behind his knees.

She'd never kissed anyone like this or been kissed so in return. He broke the kiss abruptly, and they stared at each other, their foreheads touching, their breaths coming fast. She never took her eyes from his as he reached between his legs. The anticipation was anguish as she slid closer to the edge of the desk, but she didn't blink, and neither did he.

When he entered her, they closed their eyes.

But Emily forced hers back open. He must have sensed it, because he did the same, and as he rocked into her, slowly at first, they watched each other, their bodies tightening, trembling.

Emily let it go, the rhythm of it enveloping her. Soon that cadence was all she knew, and she matched his sounds with her own.

It wasn't enough.

Mason withdrew, and even that brief sensation was enough to interrupt her ragged breaths with a burst of pleasure. Emily eased herself from the desk and responded to the guidance of his hands, turning around so that her back was against his chest, wanting to end their separation as quickly as they could.

He obliged her, and this time the feeling was doubled as the force of his driving legs lifted her to her toes. She leaned down, elbows on the desk, the fire forming a wonderful spiral inside of her. She threw herself into that flame as it made ever-widening circles. Each time he pushed into her, more of her was burned away, leaving only the feeling itself.

She didn't know if Mason called out her name or not. She heard nothing but the drumming of her own fists against the desk and perhaps the distant echo of something that had come before.

Chapter Twenty-Six

Mason pulled himself from the dream like a swimmer reaching shore.

Opening his eyes, he saw mostly darkness. Moonlight stole between the curtains, but that was all. The normally red numbers on the clock were hidden behind what Mason assumed was a random article of clothing. His shirt or hers?

He smiled and listened to her breathe.

The room smelled faintly of their sweat. He tasted her in his mouth.

For several minutes he lay there seeing and feeling and hearing it all again, the sounds they'd made, the way their bodies had intertwined like graceful dancers.

Sleep pulled him back, hoping to drag him under its waves. He slid toward it, wanting to drift wherever its undertow took him. The nearness of Emily's body intoxicated him. Perhaps if he pulled himself close enough to her, the two of them could remain here for days, doing nothing but enjoying each other's warmth. There was no need to return to whatever on earth they'd been doing before they met. He could hardly even remember that time…

He thought of the trees.

At once, sleep lost a bit of control. He came back to his senses—at least somewhat—and imagined his logging buddies sweeping down the hill and stacking the semi-trucks with the last evidence of the shepherd's existence. If there was a clue there about the location of the cave, it would be lost before they broke for lunch.

Short of sabotaging the operation, that's all I can do.

His own words returned to him. Jimmy White Cloud believed that the highest truths were revealed only in dreams. And here was his grandson, flirting with a dream quest of his own.

Short of sabotaging the operation...

He considered those words, there in the dark only inches from Emily's naked body. Just for the sake of argument, he envisioned that particular path. What if he undermined his own crew? What if he turned traitor, crept out in the night, and wrecked their saws and dozers and trucks?

Foolish. Stupid and foolish. Not to mention illegal.

The cutters would get to work at dawn. A few hours later, they would clear the quadrant. There was no way to prevent it. Could Mason simply demand to see each log they felled before they loaded them on the truck? That *might* have been feasible, except the act of sawing down the tree would probably ruin any symbol that might have been there. So that wasn't an option.

But purposefully wrecking the equipment? Could he actually *do* that?

It sounded preposterous. He would need to leave right now and use the darkness to conceal his actions as he drove up the hill and ransacked his company's property. If he left any evidence behind at all, they would find him and lock him up. This was the stuff of felonies.

He'd need a diversion.

Yes, that's how the clever movie crooks did it in Hollywood. Shift the blame elsewhere. Use a bit of misdirection so as to avoid suspicion. Could he produce such a thing?

He lifted a hand and rubbed his eyes. The fact that he was even considering taking such radical action meant he was either mostly asleep or mostly in love. It was hard to say.

He waited for ten minutes and mulled it over, staring up into the dark. He wanted to wake Emily up and tell her of his wild thoughts, or wake her up and pull her on top of him again. But instinct advised him not to rouse her. And as he lay there, the first figments of a plan began to materialize.

Could it be done?

He slowly pushed himself to a sitting position. The single white sheet was tangled around their legs. He looked at Emily. A band of moonlight rested on her bare shoulder. Mason wished that he could have introduced her to Brianna. His little sister never would have believed that he'd met a woman like this.

Time passed, and Mason felt every second. If he was going to do this outrageous thing, it had to be now.

"Then let's do it." He mouthed these words without making a sound.

Moving cautiously, he extricated himself from the sheet and covered Emily with it. He considered leaning over her just to inhale the smell of her hair, but he couldn't risk interrupting her sleep. Still, it was tempting. He'd poured himself into this woman in a way he hadn't thought possible, but instead of feeling empty for all that he'd given, he overflowed with what she'd given in return. He thought about experiencing that sensation every day for the rest of his life…

Reluctantly he pushed the thought away. For good or ill, he had business with the waiting night.

Slipping from bed, he walked silently to the bathroom but didn't turn on the light. He located jeans and shirt by touch, digging them from the hamper, and never mind how much they needed to be washed; clean clothes didn't matter at the moment. He found socks, knew they wouldn't match, and then squirted a dab of toothpaste onto his tongue. His boots were where he left them by the desk, though he didn't try and put them on until he was outside on the porch.

He looked up at the sky. In many ways it resembled the dark ceiling of his room, yet here was an endless depth of stars, tiny suns that warmed worlds he would never see. Normally that made him sad. But tonight, it gave him power.

Would she awaken when he fired up the truck?

Better not to take the chance. Fortunately, his driveway sloped downward before joining the main road. Mason got behind the wheel and softly let the door come to a rest in the frame. He'd slam it properly once he got beyond earshot. He shifted into neutral, took his foot off the clutch, and released the brake.

The truck didn't move.

Mason smirked to himself in the dark. Perhaps this was a sign that he was supposed to go back and tell Emily of his intentions. And as tempting as that was, it would mean involving her as a conspirator. He refused to put her in that kind of danger. If all of this unraveled and he ended up in jail, at least he would know that she was free.

He got out and pushed.

The big truck refused to move. But then eventually it did, inch by inch until gravity got a solid grip. Mason hopped in as it rolled. When it reached the road at the bottom of the hill, he hit the clutch and cranked the key.

Moments later he was on his way, hoping that his grandfather would speak up soon with some advice on what he was about to do. But if Jimmy White Cloud knew anything about sabotage, he kept his knowledge to himself.

****

The clock on the pickup's dashboard read 3:22, giving Mason less than three hours before dawn.

He drove through the darkness with his window rolled down. He wanted the wind in his face. It gave him the sensation of speed, reminding him of the urgency of his mission.

Mission? Is that what this was? Some kind of crazy secret mission?

"Something like that." He didn't turn on the radio because he needed to think. He didn't want to be distracted by a country love song telling him all those things he already knew about Emily. If he spent too much time thinking of her, he'd lose focus at a time when he needed it most.

He slowed when he reached the temporary track that led up the mountain. He shifted down into second gear and rumbled up the incline. If he were a proper hoodlum, he would've killed the headlights and driven the entire route in the dark so as not to be seen. But the road was too treacherous. He would have to hope that everyone within ten miles of Rockerton was still asleep.

His palms sweated despite the wind that blew through the cab. He couldn't remember the last time he'd broken the law. Even as a punk kid back in Arizona, he hadn't partaken of the usual antics. No slashing the tires of hated teachers, no tagging of public buildings with inscrutable gang signs. When he was nine he'd used a BB gun to shoot out a dozen lightbulbs just for fun, but he'd received such a whipping for it that he'd never picked up the gun again. And now what was he about to do?

"Vandalize and destroy private property."

Now that he said it, he felt a little more confident.

Didn't he?

He shut off the engine and let the truck coast to a stop. Insects filled the void with their competing songs.

He couldn't get out. Not without thinking of her again—the way she'd moved, the things her hands had done to him.

Rubbing his face, he opened the door and put his boots on the ground. Retrieving a flashlight from behind the seat, he headed toward the small trailer they used as a mobile command post, watching his steps so as not to trip in the dark. Was he walking toward his vision quest? He'd often wondered what it was like during his grandfather's day and in even earlier times when a young brave would embark on such a sojourn, wrestling with the demons he met in the wilderness and coming back a man. Was this such an adventure, or was he simply doing it as part of a lovesick delusion?

"Does it even matter?"

In the stillness, his whisper sounded louder than he intended. Luckily, he reached the trailer without snapping any twigs or otherwise causing the crickets to fall silent. Only rarely did he ever find himself deep in the woods at night, but he was comfortable enough.

There was nothing out here that meant him any harm. Even the occasional bear or wolf didn't worry him, as those grand creatures had better things to do than trouble a hapless human on what could only be called a fool's errand.

He swung the flashlight beam back and forth, looking for the toolbox.

When he finally located the big metal box, he used his key to open the padlock, then removed the bolt-cutters and purposefully cut through the lock he'd just opened. Now it would look as if someone had brought along their own cutters and forced their way in. After the lock was mangled beyond repair, he trained the light directly on it and considered what he'd done. Now there was no going back. He remembered to put on his gloves for fear of leaving prints.

The fingerprint thing amused him. You knew that you were at an exceptionally weird place in your life when you were concerned about the cops dusting for your prints.

"The things we do for love," he said to himself, then grabbed the can of paint.

The paint was the safety-orange color the loggers used to mark certain trees and the perimeter of the day's cutting zone. Officially it was known as Omaha orange. Whatever. Now it was the color of graffiti.

Mason started small, making meaningless marks across the bulldozer and portable toilet. Then he created his bit of misdirection in the form of fictional environmental activists. Across the side of the trailer he wrote TREE KILLERZ, took pride in the addition of the "Z."

But that was only the beginning. If he caused

enough havoc, the crew would be forced to shut down for the better part of the day while the police investigated. The notion of breaking windows and cutting fuel lines bothered him, though, to the point where he stood flat-footed with his flashlight pointed at the ground.

He looked up. Was there courage to be found in the stars?

His thoughts returned again to Emily. What if she woke up and found him gone?

That did it. He couldn't stand here contemplating the heavens or this ache for her in his bones. He got an axe from the tool chest and broke open the trailer door. Once inside, he went to the rack of chainsaws and systematically drained the oil from each of them, letting it run onto the floor. He tossed the oil caps through the open door. They'd never find them in the underbrush, causing further delay. That done, he raided the single filing cabinet, throwing papers about at random and wishing he had the heart to laugh at himself for what he'd become.

He shook his head and left the trailer, using the flashlight to find his way to the bulldozer. The aging Caterpillar D8K had eaten up many of his mornings since he'd signed on with the company. How many days had he planted his butt on that uncomfortable seat? Too many. He didn't experience any remorse when he gutted the thing, pulling wires and hoses from its burly diesel engine and tossing them into the trees.

That done, he went in search of further destruction.

Then he stopped, thought about his boots, and looked down. Examining his footwear in the small pool of light, he wondered if the police would know him by his tracks. Did his boots bear a distinctive tread pattern?

No, it wouldn't matter. The ground here had been crossed countless times by the entire crew. There was no way the crime-scene techs would ever focus on Mason's alone.

Was there?

Too late now, he supposed. He went to the port-a-john and pushed it over on its side. Its plastic door fell open, permitting a noxious odor to escape.

Mason backed away. Was that enough? Would it slow them down?

If the authorities got involved, then certainly their investigation would halt all activity in this quadrant...but only for a while. Emily would need to hurry.

Mason nodded once to himself and jogged back to the truck. The dashboard clock now read 4:39. He drove home quickly, hoping she was still asleep. He removed his boots on the porch, carried them inside, stripped down, and padded quietly into the bedroom.

Emily lay on her stomach. The sheet had worked its way down, uncovering her back. Moonlight fired an arrow across her shoulders.

As carefully as he could, Mason got in beside her. She moved only a little and made a faint sound. Mason hoped he could hear that sound for many nights to come. First, though, they had to get through tomorrow.

He closed his eyes but didn't sleep.

Chapter Twenty-Seven

Emily dreamed of Africa.

She ran with a lioness on the savannah. She never caught her quarry or outran what might have been pursuing her. She just ran and ran.

She came awake slowly, the hot African sky giving way to a pillow that smelled like a man. Usually her dreams were literal and required no interpretation. This one, though, had certainly been inspired by what had happened last night.

Remembering it all, she came fully to her senses.

"You're smiling," Mason said.

She smiled through a yawn. "Comes with the territory."

"You look fantastic."

She draped her arm over his bare stomach. "Flattery will get you everywhere."

Mason edged closer to her, and she snuggled against him. She had no desire to leave this warmth they'd made. The world beyond this bed could go to hell, thank you very much.

"Sweet dreams?" he asked.

"Strange ones. You?"

He said nothing.

Keeping her eyes closed, she poked him gently. "Fine, don't tell me."

"I didn't sleep much."

"I'm sorry. I think I slept enough for both of us." She'd no sooner said this than she felt herself slipping again, beckoned to that delicious state of existence where she was just awake enough to enjoy his body and dazed enough to think it would never end.

"Are you hungry?" he asked after a while.

"Eating would involve getting up."

"I could bring you breakfast in bed."

"That would involve *you* getting up, and you're not going anywhere."

Again he was silent.

Finally, she lifted her head and peered at him through the hair in her face. "You're not going anywhere, are you?"

He smiled and brushed the hair from her eyes. "You are so beautiful."

"You're going to work, aren't you?"

"I have to be there."

"Why?"

"I've played hooky too much recently."

"Resign."

"Are you going to pay my bills?"

She kissed the ridge of his abdominals.

"Anything to keep you here."

"I wish it were that easy."

"You won't know until you try." Emily couldn't remember the last time she'd felt this playful. "The only reason I might get out of this bed is to brush my teeth, and that won't take very long."

"What about the shepherd?"

"Damn the shepherd."

"You can't damn the shepherd."

"I can. It's a woman prerogative to damn any man

she pleases."

"I'll keep that in mind." He stroked her hair. "What happened to being on a tight schedule?"

"*You* happened," she said. "*We* happened. Or did you already forget?"

"Do you know what time it is?"

"Do I care?"

Mason removed her top from where it had fallen over the bedside clock.

"It's not even seven yet," Emily said, thinking that she might pout until she got her way.

"The sun is on its way up."

"Then we'll just have to keep our eyes closed." She nestled even nearer to him, her cheek resting on his stomach.

"I'm due on the site at seven-thirty."

"Will they fire you if you're late?"

"I know I said I'd quit and take a chance as a full-time woodworker and all, but I'd like to give them their two weeks."

Emily saw the sense in what he was saying. But having collided with him so completely last night, the thought of separating was too cruel for this hour of the day. Later there would be time to put it all in perspective and answer its many questions. How did this change things? What did it mean for her academic work? Would she really fly back to New Jersey?

Find me.

Emily thought she was drifting to sleep again. But that voice hadn't belonged to her dreams.

Find me, please.

"Hey," she said.

"Hmmm?"

"Sarita says I have to get up."

"I thought we damned the shepherd."

"We did. But not the love of his life." She pushed herself up on an elbow. "You're right."

"About what?"

"I need to get my ass out there and find that cave before it's too late."

"Yeah, you'll have to wear your running shoes this morning. I like it, by the way."

"Like what?"

"Your ass." He patted it twice.

"Oh, you *do*, do you?" She slid on top of him.

"Very much so."

Emily couldn't help but giggle. And when was the last time she'd done *that?* She'd assumed that giggling was no longer in her repertoire, yet here she was, as giddy as a seventeen-year-old who'd just had sex for the first time.

Mason took her face in his hands. "Seriously. You should already be out the door."

"Are you kicking me out of bed?"

"Me and Sarita both."

Emily sighed. She rested her chin on his chest. "Can we have lunch this afternoon?"

"Sure."

"You'll come find me when you get away from the chainsaws for a while?"

He was silent for a moment, and she wondered what he was thinking. Then he said, "I'll shoot for noon on the dot, but it all depends on how work is going at that particular moment. Sometimes we get in the middle of a job—"

"No excuses," she said, swinging off of him and

hunting down her clothes. "I expect to see you galloping through the woods at lunchtime." She didn't give him the chance to reply, shutting herself in the bathroom and leaning against the door.

Was it real? Had last night happened?

She shivered. Now that she was no longer in his embrace, goosebumps spread along her arms. She turned on the shower and let the steam envelop her. Though she would've normally taken her time under the hot spray, enjoying the fresh memory of their coupling, she knew that Mason was right: she had to get out there and find whatever dendroglyphs remained undiscovered. So she dressed in yesterday's clothes, did as little as possible with her hair—it wasn't as awful as it could've been, but it wasn't great—then left the bathroom with his name on her lips.

He was gone.

"Mason?"

If he'd already left, Emily would have to call Tunny to get a ride back to camp. That was no big deal, of course, but she'd been hoping to ride shotgun with Mason driving, just so she could hear him talk about nature spirits and the books he'd read. She roamed the house but found only a note on the kitchen table. She read its single line: CAN'T WAIT TO SHARE MORE ECHOES WITH YOU.

Emily read it again and shook her head at her own fantastic fortune. But a small part of her couldn't help but wonder when that fortune would run out.

****

Mason saw them even before he stopped the truck. The members of his crew stood like observers at a natural disaster, hands on their hips, hats tipped back.

He got out and slowly approached them.

His destruction appeared different in the daylight.

The bright orange paint looked worse than everyday graffiti. It screamed out a warning, so that he could almost hear an environmentalist shouting it at him—*Treekillerz!* The men took in the sight with incredulous faces. Nothing like this had ever happened here before, not around the normally somnolent village of Rockerton, Colorado.

Luiz stepped from the trailer with a chainsaw in hand. "Looks like they got 'em all. Drained the damn things dry." His voice held no anger, only bafflement. "Can't find the caps anywhere."

No one replied. They looked from the upturned toilet to the wires sticking from the dozer's engine.

"Reckon they're still around?" someone asked.

"You mean watchin' us from the trees?"

Jim Hartlet approached the bulldozer. He'd always had a fondness for it; at one point he'd named it Darla. "Kids do this, you think? Mason?"

Mason had been so consumed by thoughts of Emily that he'd failed to prepare a bit of artifice to get him through the next few hours. "Uh, this doesn't look like kids to me."

"Then who the hell did it?"

"Evidently someone who doesn't like what we're doing up here."

"Half the damn town is full of logger families!"

"I don't know what to tell you, Jim."

Hartlet inspected the damage to the engine. "Probably peace-niks from Boulder."

Mason walked toward the trailer and pretended to study the spray-painted letters. In reality, he was breathing deliberately in an effort to look nonchalant. He'd never crossed the legal line before, and now that he was here, he was uncertain how to handle himself.

"Hey, Mace," Luiz said. "What should we do?"

Mason hooked a thumb in his jeans pocket. "Call the foreman, I guess."

"I'm on it."

While they waited on the chief to drive down from the company HQ, the men took advantage of the situation by lighting up cigarettes and making seats of truck tailgates. Somebody returned the portable toilet to an upright position, their boots further obscuring any tracks Mason might have left behind when he pushed it over four hours ago.

"Darla ain't as bad off as I thought," Hartlet said. "The bastards only broke a nail and scuffed some of her makeup. Somebody fire her up and let me have a look."

Mason glanced around. Because the rest of the crew had wandered away, he happened to be the closest to the bulldozer. He had no choice but to hop up behind the controls.

"Boss is on his way!" Luiz announced.

Mason knew that he'd fail a polygraph if it came down to that. But of course that was ludicrous. No one would ever suspect him.

Would they?

"What are you waitin' for, Mace? Crank her up."

Mason obliged, turning the key and bringing the big diesel to life—

Flames erupted from the engine.

The fire reached out like an arm, snaring Hartlet around the head. He screamed and stumbled backward. His knees dropped out from under him, and he fell, holding his face with both hands. "My eyes!"

Mason immediately turned off the engine and jumped down. "Jim!"

"I'm burned, holy shit, I'm burned!"

The men ran toward them. Mason, seized by a kind of panic he'd never experienced, hovered over his friend but didn't know what to do. Hartlet wasn't on fire, but the scent of vaporized hair was unmistakable.

The rest of the crew raced toward them, forming a circle around their fallen friend. Mason could hardly breathe, his throat was clogged with guilt. He took Hartlet by the wrists and forced the words out. "Move your hands, let me see."

"It hurts!"

"Move your hands."

Hartlet uncovered his eyes. The skin on his forehead and temples was hairless and pink. His eyebrows had been burned away. The damage wasn't as bad as Mason had feared, but it was enough.

"What do we do?" someone shouted.

Mason swallowed as best he could. "Call an ambulance." He coughed twice. "And the cops. Get them up here, *now*." Though he'd originally planned to delay the police's arrival for as long as possible, giving Emily as much time as he could before they began their investigation, now his primary concern was Hartlet. If the man was seriously injured, Mason didn't know what he would do.

Luiz yelled into the radio. Hartlet lay on his back, arms over his face, jaw clenched against the pain. The men took off their hats and cursed whoever had brought this upon them. Mason silently joined them, hating himself for what he'd done.

Chapter Twenty-Eight

Emily held a perfect leaf in her hand. She'd never seen one so flawless, as delicate as a snowflake. This morning, everything was new to her. This leaf had drifted down as she was examining a trunk. She'd taken that as a token that all was well.

Did she love him?

It was too early to say. She wanted simply to enjoy this pre-relationship glow, when she was uncertain about the future but uncertain in a good way. Would they stay together forever or fall to pieces next Tuesday? Right now, she didn't care. Everything about him seemed like this leaf.

Unfortunately, her delightful mood had rendered her a terrible researcher. She went from tree to tree as usual, but she no longer bothered with her fieldbook and GPS. Her concentration ebbed. She was too busy thinking of last night and wondering if there would be a sequel this evening.

She waited for Magnelli's voice to speak up and call her a silly girl, but the old prof apparently knew when he was up against an insurmountable foe. There would be no dislodging Mason from her thoughts.

She worked for half an hour but found nothing other than some raccoon scratches and a particularly interesting centipede. And the leaf, of course, her fallen omen of good things to come.

A new sound rose in the distance.

Emily stood up straight. What was it? A noise she hadn't heard since she left Jersey...

"Sirens."

The sound was out of place in these woods. Had someone started a forest fire?

Fire reminded her of last night. At one point she'd felt as if she were going to burst into flames. She would've been happy to have died that way, consumed by pleasure.

Blinking, she returned from her reverie to hear the sirens had drawn closer. They sounded no farther than a hundred yards away. And that meant they were headed toward the logging crew.

"Mason?"

Had something happened to him? In an instant she imagined the worst: the morning after sleeping with the most desirable man she'd ever met, she would lose him to a falling tree or a wayward saw.

She forgot everything about the dendroglyphs and ran through the trees, wanting only to see his face.

****

Two paramedics who looked barely out of college tended to the wounded man, while Emily held Mason's hand as if it were a lifeline. She marveled at their youth. One white, one black, they were as fit and charming as TV actors playing the part of EMTs. One of them applied strips of gauze to the man's burns while the other used a stylus to add notes to a tablet in a protective plastic case. Though the sirens no longer blared, the lights of their ambulance continued to flash.

"How did it happen?" she asked.

He didn't respond immediately, but watched the

sheriff who was busy interviewing the crew. The sheriff had strong Hispanic features but no hint of an accent. He wore a cowboy hat. Did all lawmen west of Indiana wear cowboy hats?

"Mason, talk to me."

"Sorry. When I started the dozer, there was...there was some kind of brief electrical fire. I did something that...I don't know..."

"It's not your fault."

Mason stood silently.

The company foreman stalked about in obvious anger. Emily recognized him. She'd encountered him at the Cross Cut a week ago. He was one of the men who'd challenged her about her profession and inspired her to make her public declaration. Mason had said his name was Larry Ellsworth. He followed a deputy who took photos of the vandalism.

"You know what I'm thinking here?" Ellsworth said loudly enough for everyone to hear. "I'm thinking this was eco-terrorists."

"Let's not start making any assumptions," the deputy advised, calmly recording the evidence. "That won't help anybody."

"They're up here, you know," Ellsworth went on. "Maybe they call themselves environmentalists, but just between you and me and the fencepost, I bet that most of them are radicals. You ever hear of tree-spiking?"

The deputy said something that Emily couldn't hear. She looked at Mason. "I take it that this has never happened before."

He shook his head.

"Is he going to be okay?"

"The medics seemed to think so. He's not blind,

that's the main thing."

"Hey, this has really gotten you shaken up."

He gestured as if to say it was no big deal, when clearly it was.

"Just because you're the one who turned on the engine doesn't mean it was your fault."

Mason gathered a breath, held it, then let it out slowly.

In the brief time that Emily had known him, she'd never seen him like this. He was taking the blame for what had happened. The foreman had put him in charge of the crew. It was his responsibility. "I know what you're thinking," she said.

"You do?"

"The captain goes down with his ship and all of that stuff. It's good that you're concerned, but that doesn't mean you should be wishing you could trade places with him."

Mason didn't look convinced.

The sheriff headed toward them. He wasn't a large man, but there was something about him that had a visible effect on the crew. Maybe it was just the power of his badge, but they gave him a wide berth. He stopped in front of Mason. His brass name plate read WILLIAM GARZA. "Good morning, Mr. Hitapwa."

"Sheriff."

He removed his hat and extended a hand to Emily. "Bill Garza."

She introduced herself and shook.

"A pleasure," he said. "You're the one writing the book?"

"The book?"

"Rumor is that you're here writing a local history.

Then again, I should know by now not to listen to gossip, especially when it's coming from my own deputies. They're worse than old wives."

"Well, that's somewhat accurate. I'm working on my doctoral dissertation."

"Ah. Well, that's too bad. The fact that my deputies were discussing books was encouraging. They're the type that usually wait for the movie version."

Emily smiled, instantly liking this man with the craggy face and gentle manner. "If I ever get it published, I'll be sure to send them a copy."

"Please." He turned to Mason. "Mr. Ellsworth is ranting about terrorists."

"Yes, sir. I heard."

"Dangerous stuff."

"Yes."

"Do you agree with him?"

Emily watched Mason as he glanced around at the damage. She sensed his unease and felt the rigidness of his stance. "If Jim hadn't gotten hurt, I'd say it was no big deal. The most annoying thing is having to buy new oil caps for the saws."

"So these weren't very terrorizing terrorists," Garza said.

"Comparatively speaking, no."

The sheriff rested his hands on his utility belt in what Emily guessed was a posture he often assumed. The gun in his holster wasn't anything flashy, but a revolver, just the kind of thing she expected from a Wild West lawman. "Don't take this the wrong way," he said, "but the men here probably ended this investigation before I even got here."

"I don't follow."

He motioned to the forest floor. "They walked all over the evidence. In a perfect world, we could've found markings from the soles of the bad guys' shoes. And I'm also not very hopeful as far as fingerprints are concerned."

"I'm sorry. We didn't think about it."

"No worries. But your boss won't be happy when we tell him that we have little chance of finding his vandals. Unless someone comes forward with information..." He shrugged.

"Is Jim going to be all right?"

Garza glanced back at the ambulance. "They tell me he has only first-degree burns. He lost some hair and some pride, but other than that, I think he'll recover just fine."

Emily felt Mason relax, but only a little. "That's good."

"Good until the feds get here, anyway."

Emily thought she'd misheard that. "Pardon me?"

"The *federales*, Ms. Radsco. There was a time when we could've handled this locally, but these days, if anyone so much as whispers about terrorists, even the environmental kind, I'm obligated to make a call to my colleagues at the Department of Homeland Security."

Mason shifted his weight from one foot to the other. "The federal government will be investigating this?"

"That's not necessarily as heavy-duty as it sounds," Garza said. "It's not like they're going to dispatch a helicopter full of top agents from D.C. They'll send a couple of rookies who'll ask a few questions and end up drawing the same conclusions that the rest of us have already drawn."

"And what conclusions are those?"

"That this is too small-time to lose much sleep over. Maybe a couple hundred bucks in damages and a few days off work for Mr. Hartlet there."

"That's it?"

"Unless somebody gives us a tip, I reckon it is." He cast another glance across the scene, taking it all in. "Or maybe it's not."

She didn't like the sound of that. "Meaning what?"

"You never know, Ms. Radsco. Sometimes clues turn up in the damndest places. Good to meet you, ma'am. Mason."

Mason nodded. "Bill."

Emily watched him as he slowly walked the ground between the trailer and the bulldozer. His deputies strung yellow tape between the trees that formed the perimeter. "You know," she said, "it looks like something good might come from this, after all."

"Oh, yeah?"

"It doesn't seem as if they'll be cutting anything else here today."

"That's probably true."

"And that's good news, right?" She tugged his arm. "Hey, what's the matter? Your friend is going to be fine, and you and I get one more uninterrupted day to find any more surprises from Sarita's lover."

Mason silently appraised the situation.

"I like the strong, silent type as much as the next girl," Emily said, "but it also wouldn't kill you to talk to me about whatever's bothering you."

He smiled, but only a little. "I'll go ask Larry what he's planning for the rest of the day. Hopefully he'll tell us all to head on home."

Emily let him go, never taking her eyes off him. The morning's events had shaken him, sapping some of the confidence that Emily had grown to admire. What could she do to help him stop blaming himself and forget about it?

A few things came to mind, and she grinned.

"Hurry up," she whispered, wanting him back at her side.

Chapter Twenty-Nine

They spent the morning like spirits moving between the silver aspens, touching whenever they passed. Ellsworth had shut things down for the day, giving Garza's men room to operate, planting their little flags in the earth and taking endless photos. Less than fifty yards away from where the deputies now worked, Mason listened to Emily talk about whatever was on her mind. He contributed just enough to the conversation to make her believe he wasn't torn with worry.

Because of him, Hartlet had been injured. True, the man's wounds would heal without lasting damage, but still, it could've been much worse.

And now the feds were on the way. Mason was a man who'd always stayed well on the right side of the legal line. Even as a teenager, his rebellions had been mild. He'd never served community service for firing bottle rockets at the neighbor's car. But now? Now he was the object of a federal investigation, even if the investigators themselves were unaware of it.

"Is it lunchtime yet?" Emily asked.

Mason found her leaning against a tree. He touched her hair, pulling a few strands of it through his fingers. "It's still early."

"A woman needs to eat."

"Didn't the woman have breakfast?"

She put her arms around his neck. "I've burned a lot of calories this morning. Playing around in the woods with you is really exhausting."

He kissed her. It felt so nice.

"If you're trying to distract me from my rumbling tummy," she said, "it's working."

Mason wondered how long he could hold her, kiss her, breathe the scent of her hair. And instead of keeping these thoughts to himself, he decided to tell her. Right now, he needed her more than he did last night. "I wish this forest went on forever," he said, his face inches from hers. "Being with you here, looking for hidden words on trees...it's like I'm in the middle of a story my grandfather might have told."

Her eyes glowed when she smiled. "And what would your grandfather have said about us?"

Mason thought about it. "Well, he would've started with a description of how the world was before men came. That's how all of his stories began. So before men and women came to these woods, there was a deer—a buck with a wild rack of antlers." He put his hands on his head as if they were horns. "And he roamed the forest and ate its sweet grass and spent most of his time alone."

Emily looked up at him, rapt, saying nothing.

"One day his aloneness was interrupted by a doe."

"Uh, oh."

"It's true. The buck saw her from a distance. She moved between the trees as if searching for something. The buck knew she was special because her eyes weren't brown like the others, but green like the forest itself. Green like life."

He paused, thinking Emily might interject

something here, but she only gazed up at him.

"The buck had no choice but to chase her. He couldn't help it. Sky Father sent a wind that got tangled in the buck's antlers, and the wind carried him toward the doe. She proved too nimble to catch, darting back and forth, always a few feet in front of him, always looking for what she was sure the forest concealed. They went on like that for days, until they were both worn out, too tired to go any farther. By now they were deep in the heart of the forest, and the buck had lost his bearings. He no longer knew the way home. And neither did she. So they joined together to survive."

Emily stepped closer to him, their bodies touching.

Mason didn't know where his story was leading or what, exactly, had inspired it. But like the buck chasing the doe, he followed wherever it led. "One day they finally reached a glade, an open clearing that no human had ever trespassed upon. And do you know what was there?"

"Tell me."

"A cave. A cave like nothing they'd ever seen before. A cave full of the secrets of their ancestors, of all the wisdom they'd left behind. And so it became the responsibility of the buck and doe to collect that knowledge, and make use of it, and pass it on to all those who came after them. But you know what else?"

"What?"

"The most special of these secrets was one that the buck and doe had already learned. They knew to come together in order to find what they were seeking. Some things you can't do alone."

"I agree," she said softly. "Some things are definitely better when you don't do them by yourself."

Despite his distress over Hartlet's injury and the federal investigators, Mason couldn't help but smile. He brushed his lips across hers. "Now, I never said anything in that story about the buck and doe hooking up as a romantic couple."

"Sorry, I just assumed." She didn't look sorry.

"There was no deer mating going on in those woods."

"Somehow I find that hard to believe. Boy deer meets girl deer...they usually end up snuggling."

"Snuggling?"

"And it kind of evolves from there."

He kissed her forehead, well aware of the pressure of her body against his. "They probably had too much on their minds to worry about doing that sort of thing."

She explored him with her hands, deftly unfastening the top button of his jeans. "Doesn't sound like a very entertaining story when you tell it that way."

"It's rated G."

"Is it? Right now, I don't think I'm interested in rated G." There went the second and third buttons.

Mason could barely resist. He wanted to drag her to the ground and expel this sudden fire that was burning him up at her touch. But right here? Right now? "Too bad we're so close."

"Uh, I think closeness is kind of necessary for this sort of thing."

"I mean to the crew. Larry may have sent everyone home, but the deputies are probably still finishing up."

"What they don't know won't hurt them."

"They're not very far away."

"Then we'll just have to be extremely quiet."

"Stealth-mode sex?"

She grinned. "Right under their radar."

****

The afternoon sun pushed the shadows of the aspens farther along the forest floor. The air assumed that golden quality of coming dusk, the leaves outlined by the last of the day's light. The stillness was as complete as any Emily had known since venturing to this place. Even the squirrels and birds had settled down.

She stood up and massaged her lower back. Mason worked forty feet down the hill, searching the trees. Emily watched him move between the branches.

Why had he been so quiet today?

Emily wondered if she were making him nervous. Was she coming on too strong? The last thing she wanted was to frighten him off. But she'd never felt this way before. It was difficult for her to control her emotions, so what chance did she have of playing hard to get? And why the hell would she want to?

"Do try and stay focused, dear." She said this to herself with half a smile. Her research was important to her, but this afternoon she'd given more thought to Mason than she had to her dissertation. Her work had gotten sloppy, and this would no doubt be reflected in the final product.

She made her way down the hill.

They'd found nothing today. If the shepherd had secreted any additional clues in the woodwork, Emily and Mason had been unable to tease them out. Maybe all of this would turn out to be pointless. Maybe Sarita would remain only a name, her fate never known. Emily wished for some kind of time machine to take her back, so that she could watch Sarita from afar or perhaps introduce herself. The two of them could stand on either side of a clothesline, talking of the weather and local gossip and invariably of men.

As she approached Mason, she reached out a hand. He accepted it without speaking. They stood for a while watching twilight lay claim to the forest.

Eventually Emily said, "I think this is turning out to be a lost cause."

"Never say die."

"Doctoral candidates are by nature skeptical of anything that can't be verified. And right now, this cave definitely falls into that category."

"Are you kidding?" He swept his arm in such a way to encompass the entire range of connected hills. "We still have about two and a half million trees to check."

"I appreciate your ambition, but honestly I'm no longer keeping the faith."

Still holding her hand, he stepped in front of her so he could look directly at her. "Are you giving up?"

"I'm just saying there may be more important things."

"Like us?"

She shrugged, not wanting to give away too much of her heart. "Maybe."

"What if we recruited some more help? If we had enough people walking the woods—"

"That's a lot of ground to cover."

"So we'll cover it. Listen, the shepherd mentioned meeting her at a special place. There's a chance that I was wrong about that place being a cave. If we stepped back, studied the topographical maps and the history records, maybe we'd decide that it *wasn't* a cave. We could be totally overlooking something obvious."

"Do you think?"

"I don't know. But I'm not ready to give up yet, not after…"

"Not after what?"

He wet his lips, and Emily sensed he was stalling. But why?

"It's been a rough day," he finally said. "The crew will be back at it tomorrow."

"Let them. We've inspected every tree in this immediate area. The lumberjacks can saw them all to pieces. It won't make a difference."

"Why are you like this all of a sudden?"

"Me? What about you, good sir? You've been anxious all day. You're practically sprinting from one tree to the next. Suddenly I'm the realist and you're the one who's obsessed."

"I'm not obsessed."

"*Worried*, then. You look worried that if we don't find this cave that might not be a cave, then I'll just hop the first plane back to Jersey. Is that it?"

He looked at the ground. "Something like that."

She took his other hand and held both of them tightly. "Whatever it is that you want to say, just say it. You're not going to scare me away. There was a time in my life when I bent like a willow in the wind whenever things got tough, but I assure you that I'm not the same person I was back then. Things matter to me now. Solid things. And that's what this is. So, Mister Solid, spill your guts."

He thought about it for a long time before responding. "What if I told you…what if I told you that my impulse is to turn around and run as fast and far as possible?"

"Why would you feel that way? Have I done something wrong?"

"You've done everything right. It's so right that I can't take three breaths without thinking about you. About us. I've never felt this way about anyone."

"Then what's the problem? Why would you feel like running away?"

"Because…because I think the police might be chasing me."

Nothing he could have said would have surprised Emily more than this. Immediately she doubted everything she felt. She didn't know this man, after all. He had a hidden past. He was a tax evader or a drug smuggler—or worse. In moments, a hundred different possibilities occurred to her. Could she have been so wrong about him?

"It's not what you think," he said.

This did little to assuage her sudden anxiety. She slid her hands from his and crossed her arms over her chest. "I honestly have no idea *what* to think. You have about eight seconds to explain yourself before I—"

"I was the one who did it."

"Did *what?*"

"I vandalized the bulldozer and the saws. I spray-painted those words on the trailer."

Emily blinked. She let that filter through her system. Had she misheard him? "You wrecked your own company's operation?"

He nodded and looked away.

"To slow them down?"

He nodded again.

"When? You've been with me every second. Or

have I just imagined our naked bodies crushed together multiple times in the last twenty-four hours?"

"Last night. When you were asleep. It took only an hour or so."

"You snuck out?"

"It was the only thing I could do. I wanted us to find the trees. And that wasn't going to happen if the crew got busy this morning. If I hadn't done it, we wouldn't be standing here right now. See all these trees around us? They'd all be gone."

Of all the responses Emily could have given to this revelation, the one that surprised her most was her own laughter. It came from her like the opening of a pressure valve, releasing all the crazy thoughts she'd been entertaining.

"What's so funny?" he asked, looking perplexed.

"You're not a drug smuggler."

"Not that I'm aware of."

"And you don't have a secret wife and fourteen kids back in Arizona."

"What the hell are you talking about?"

She touched his face, her uncertainty having given way to a weird sort of pride. "You did this for me?"

"For us."

"You spray-painted a misspelled word on a lumberjack trailer for us?"

"I'm pretty mellow when it comes to vandalism."

"Why didn't you tell me?"

"I'm telling you now."

"You know what I mean. Why didn't you wake me up instead of slinking off in the middle of the night?"

"What would you have said?"

"I would've talked you out of it." She enjoyed the

look on his face. Had he done something stupid and illegal? Without a doubt. But as far as crimes went, it was bush-league stuff, and besides—he'd done it for her. For *them*. "I appreciate the sentiment. I really do. Nobody's ever knocked over a port-a-potty for me before, and I'm not making light of it when I say that. I think it's cool. But would I have tried to convince you not to do it? Yes. It wouldn't have made much difference if they'd cut everything down. We haven't been able to find any more carvings."

He nodded. "Yeah. In hindsight it wasn't one my best ideas. And Hartlet could've gotten seriously hurt. I feel like I want to apologize to him…"

"He's going to be fine."

"But still."

"I know." She pulled him close. "But still."

Mason held her. After a while, he said, "So what happens next?"

"We hide from the cops, I guess."

"I hope it doesn't come to that."

"As long as you didn't leave behind any incriminating DNA, I think we'll be all right."

Mason didn't reply, as if he wasn't ready to jump on her optimism bandwagon.

"Hey." She looked up at him. "I don't want to run you off by saying this, but what we have here is probably the sweetest thing that's happened to me in a long time. And if you think I'm going to let one little FBI investigation get in the way of that, you're wrong."

"You're now an accessory, you know."

"Great. Then we can be Bonnie and Clyde. Sounds fun, huh?"

"Sure, except for the part when Bonnie and Clyde

get shot down in a hail of gunfire."

"We'll try to avoid that part."

He kissed her forehead. "Okay, Bonnie, I'll trust you. But what about the trees? Everything in this area is likely to be gone by tomorrow evening. And we haven't found anything yet. I'm afraid the shepherd may be lost."

"He can't be lost." She said it in defiance, though looking around the darkening wood, she suspected that it might be true.

Chapter Thirty

Lightning bugs signaled from the darkness, blinking a few feet from the cabin's porch.

Emily typed.

Sitting in a rocking chair with her laptop, she stared into the white glow of the monitor and recorded her thoughts as they came to her, if only because Magnelli required weekly updates of her progress. Every time she looked up, she saw only darkness, as the computer screen ruined her night vision. If not for the tiny strobes of the fireflies, she would have seen nothing at all.

Mason showered. Emily heard the falling water through the wall. She'd been tempted to join him and would've accepted the offer had he made it, but he was still subdued, troubled by how close he'd come to blinding his friend.

Emily wrote, *I am ga-ga for a vandal.* That brought a crooked smile to her face.

If someone had asked her to describe her ideal man, she probably wouldn't have named any traits that Mason possessed. Sure, he was dark-eyed and had an athlete's body, but physical lusciousness aside, he didn't meet many of her preconceived criteria. Was he a college graduate? Was he upwardly mobile? No on both accounts, yet he was self-educated and well-read, and he replaced career aspirations with the desire to live fully in the moment. He made beautiful things. He valued truth more than money, and he knew the names of the stars and how to do magic tricks with quarters. And he baked his own bread.

She added another line: *Is ga-ga enough?*

There were levels of love. Years ago, before she'd gotten her head on straight, she'd moved through relationships irresponsibly, but those liaisons had taught her the value of keeping things in clear layers. She could always tell the friendship layers from the deeper stuff, and that allowed her to avoid a lot of heartache in between.

So where was this one at?

Way down there, she wrote. She couldn't sit for three minutes without thinking of him.

The on-and-off switches of the lightning bugs made a pattern that Emily tried unsuccessfully to interpret. She wished they would lead her to the shepherd's final messages...if indeed any such messages existed.

She closed the laptop's lid and let her eyes make sense of the night. An image came to her—Mason's naked body with sudsy water running down his skin.

"Yeah, ga-ga is enough." Smiling at herself, she got up and went back in the cabin just as the telephone rang.

Mason was still in the shower. Emily looked to the land-line phone near the fridge and considered answering it for him, for no other reason than to feel what it was like to be so casual in his house and to use a phone that was connected to the wall by an actual cord. She came to her senses and set her laptop on the counter. From here, she had a clear line of sight on the phone's caller ID screen: COUNTY SHER OFF.

County sher off?

"Sheriff's office," she said, freezing where she stood. Why would they call at this hour? Maybe there was no reason to panic. Maybe Mason was friends with a dispatcher who was calling to chat about the Avalanche's odds of winning the Stanley Cup this year. Or maybe they wanted to talk about the—

"Something wrong?"

Emily turned to see Mason standing framed in the bathroom doorway, wearing only a pale blue towel. He was mostly dry, save a line of moisture like a necklace at his throat.

"Emily?"

"You look great," she said, meaning it.

"Why do you look like I just caught you stealing my silverware?"

She pointed at phone. "This might be bad news."

With the shadow of concern passing over his face, he went to the counter where the phone waited, one hand holding his towel in place.

"I don't suppose you regularly receive calls from the sheriff's department," she said.

"Only during the holidays when they're collecting donations for the children's fund." He stared down at the phone, tapping his knuckles on a counter top he'd likely made himself. "Guess I need to call them back."

"Yeah." She settled onto the nearest bar stool. "Guess so."

He sighed, picked up the handset, and punched the call-back button.

Emily waited. She dreaded what he might hear in the pending conversation, but at the same time, her eyes played over his body, dividing her thoughts. Working with an axe and saw had hardened his chest and upper arms, yet he wasn't bulky. His movements came effortlessly. He was probably a hell of a dancer.

"This is Hitapwa," he said into the phone. "Mason Hitapwa. I just received a call from this number."

Emily sat silently, gleaning what she could from only one side of the conversation.

"Yes, that's correct," Mason said.

His actions had been against the law. Though he hadn't wrought much damage, even a little bit of paint and some lost oil caps qualified him as a criminal. Perhaps it was only misdemeanor territory, rather than a felony, but that was beside the point.

"Uh, a little after six, I think. It was early."

Did Emily really want to hitch her wagon to this star? Years ago, she'd fraternized with various Bohemian types who dabbled in soft core drugs. But no one had ever gotten hurt.

"No. Jim Hartlet wanted someone to try the engine. The damage wasn't bad. He thought he could fix it."

But Mason had done it for her. For *them*. That's how badly he wanted to know the ending of the shepherd's story.

"I didn't see anyone, if that's what you mean. No, nothing like that. What? Oh, sure, of course. You know how it is up there. Same song, different verse."

Emily wondered if the tightness in Mason's voice was as apparent to the person on the other end of the line as it was to her. He gripped the phone so rigidly that the veins stood out in his forearm.

"I will, certainly, you bet. Thanks. You, too." He ended the call and dropped the handset to the counter.

His wet hair hung in his eyes.

"Well?" Emily prompted.

"I think we're okay."

"What did they say?"

"They asked if I'd seen anyone around, anyone I didn't recognize."

"And what about you? They didn't ask you to confirm your whereabouts last night?"

He shook his head.

"So…you didn't sense that they're suspecting you of anything?"

"No."

"Or me?" she asked. "I'm new around here and known to be wandering around in the woods. Maybe I'm on the suspect list?"

"I don't think so."

Emily relaxed, if only a little.

"That was probably one of the dumber things I've done in my life," he said.

"It wasn't so bad."

"It could've been."

"But it *wasn't*. If you feel that bad about it, we can sneak back up there tonight and repaint the trailer."

He looked at her to see if she was kidding, and she was. "You know what I'd like to do right now?"

"Drop your towel?"

He laughed. "That's not what I was thinking, but I suppose I could."

"Whatever it is, you have to promise to take me with you."

"Ice cream."

She raised both eyebrows. "At this hour?"

"I have some in the freezer."

"Is this something you normally do on days when you're harassed by the cops?"

"That's why I keep it around. To subdue my sorrows with rocky road ice cream."

"I've been known to pig out on rocky road from time to time. But I never share a spoon with strange men in towels."

"You can have your own spoon."

"I think you're missing the point, big guy. It's the towel I'm after."

She kissed him and forgot all about the police and woodland messages still unfound.

Chapter Thirty-One

The crew resumed cutting in the morning.

Mason arrived to find the bulldozer repaired. The damage he'd inflicted on it was minimal, and shortly after six A.M., it was once again busy clearing deadfall from the path. The men worked as if nothing had transpired yesterday. One of them had found some white paint and slowly eradicated Mason's treekillerz.

A single strip of yellow police tape remained, hanging from a tree and occasionally turning over in the breeze.

"Thank God tomorrow's Saturday, huh, Mace?"

"Right on, Luiz."

"You got plans for the weekend?"

"My plan is to have as few plans as possible."

"I hear you on that one. My old lady, man, I don't know *where* she finds so many things for me to do. I think she just sits at home *dreaming* that crap up. You know what I mean?"

"And you love every minute of it."

"Maybe I do. Hey, are we gonna knock out this quadrant today or what?"

Mason felt that question more profoundly than Luiz would ever know. "I guess we will."

"Cool. Then let's get it on."

They worked for an hour. Mason tried to pour himself into his labors, concentrating on finishing the job, but his imagination was too powerful an opponent. He and Emily had done it in his favorite reading chair last night. Prior to that, it had seemed like an innocent place, where he'd sit for hours with the television turned off, reading intricate spy novels or social satires or poetry so old the pages smelled of dust. He'd seen the world from that chair—or at least he thought he'd seen it. Last night she took him somewhere new, straddling him, rocking up and down and then throwing back her head like a rain goddess waiting for the storm.

Mason looked up from his work and waited for the image to fade. Just how dangerous was it to operate heavy machinery and daydream at the same time?

He noticed the new guy, Hammond, working the quadrant's edge. As recently as twelve hours ago, that had been the site of Emily's camp. Yesterday evening she and Mason had disassembled her tent and packed up her little stove and Coleman lantern. The only things she left behind were her trees.

"Yo, Ham!" Mason jumped down from the bulldozer's seat. "Hammond, hold up!"

Hammond turned, chainsaw in hand. His goggles were smeared. "What's up?"

Mason walked a circle around the tree that Hammond was getting ready to fell. He glanced at the well-walked area where Emily's tent had been pitched, then nodded to himself. Yes, this was the place. They'd been naked at this tree, moving back and forth as quietly as they could in the grass.

"You mind if I do this one?" Mason asked.

"Uh, why?"

"I don't have much chance to drop one of these anymore."

He handed over the big saw."Knock yourself out."

"Go have a smoke."

"Don't have to tell me twice." Hammond hurried away, tapping his cigarette pack against his palm.

Mason's goggles dangled around his neck. He slid them into place. He didn't want to take this tree down. He wanted it to stand forever as a monument to what had transpired at its base. In that way, he supposed, he was very much like the shepherd, trying to take love and transport it into the future, so that everyone would know how special it had been.

He fired up the saw.

Guilt crept up on him. Logic told him that cutting down this tree was not symbolic of his relationship with Emily, nor would it have any impact on their ability to locate any final messages from the past. He and Emily had searched everything in the area—aspens and other species—and had discovered no further symbols or hidden notes. Removing this tree would have no negative impact on either their relationship or their quest to conclude the shepherd's story. Yet still he couldn't lift the damn saw.

"Mason, let's do this thing!"

He looked up to see Trey standing with the guide line about sixty feet away. Though the angle of Mason's cuts would force the tree to fall in the direction he intended, Trey was there as insurance. The other end of his rope was fixed midway up the tree.

Trey threw up his arms in unmistakable body language: *What are you waiting for?*

"I'm sorry, Emily." He didn't know why he was apologizing, but as the teeth bit ferociously into the bark, he cursed himself for his inability to locate that cave. Now he felt as if he'd never get the chance.

As he worked the churning blades deeper into the wood, he vowed this would be his last. He would never to cut down another tree.

****

Emily slept till eight in the morning, waking up with her face against a pillow that smelled nothing like her pillow back home. Mason's scent was the first piece of evidence that she hadn't been dreaming all of this. Perhaps she'd never left Newark for Colorado, and when she opened her eyes she'd see the clock and realize she was late for teaching the latest class Magnelli had passed off on her. But this didn't smell like her apartment.

She opened her eyes.

Light filled the window, revealing a room that was as comfortable as it was simple. The headboard of the queen-sized bed had been made by hand. The rug on the hardwood floor was in the Southwest style; Mason had bartered for it before leaving the Hopi reservation in Arizona. Last night—after their antics in a living-room chair—Mason had brought her to the bedroom and answered every question she asked. She wanted to know everything about him. She'd fallen asleep with her head on his stomach.

She sat up, yawned, and grimaced when she realized how badly she needed a toothbrush. By now Mason's crew was well on its way to erasing the last pieces of the puzzle that so obsessed her. What did that mean for the two of them? How would it affect her scholarly work? With the trees gone, what reason did Emily have for staying here?

"Decision time, old girl." She got out of bed and

purposefully avoided making any decisions for the next hour. There would be time enough for that after a shower and coffee.

When that shower was finally concluded and the blessed caffeine was moving through her blood, she couldn't avoid decisions any longer, so she made one. She called Tunny and asked for a ride to the library, where she intended to spend at least part of the day.

"Pick you up at noon for some lunch, professor?" he asked as she hopped from his truck.

"I'm not a professor yet."

"Okay, how about a professor in the making? You want me to swing by and take you to get a meatball sub or something? You're not, like, a vegan or anything, are you?"

She smiled. "Noon sounds fine. And no, I'm not."

"Great, see you then!" He honked and waved as he pulled away.

Emily situated the strap of her bag so that it wasn't digging into her shoulder, then clipped up the steps. Libraries had always been like church to her. The stillness and the proximity of so much wisdom made her feel like she was walking through a sacred space. She claimed a table in the back corner, plugged in her laptop so as not to tax the battery, and spent the next few hours recording further details of the town's history, its families, and its economic development. If the forests were giving up no more secrets, she had to salvage what she could of her now incomplete thesis. For a while she had the luxury of simply being a student again, and it calmed her, though frequent thoughts of Mason intervened.

Tunny showed up as scheduled and spent the ride

to the sub shop telling her about the high school football team and what chances they had of going all the way. Apparently the quarterback was only a sophomore, but his father had once started for the Colorado Buffalos, which was a good sign, and through all of this Emily wondered what it would've been like to be a woman in this town a century ago. What social events had been important? What was the gossip that you traded with your girlfriends?

"You're not hearin' a word I'm sayin', are you?"

She looked over, a little embarrassed. "I'm sorry. I guess I just have a lot on my mind."

"Like what?"

"Actually at that moment I was thinking about a woman."

"Anybody in particular?"

"Yes. Her name was Sarita. I never met her, but I've learned a little bit about her these last few days, though not as much as I'd like."

"I know a Sarita."

Emily narrowed her eyes. "You do? That's not a very common name."

"Sure, little Sarita Thomas. She's in my granddaughter's class, the fourth grade."

"Oh. Maybe it's more common than I thought." Emily rode in silence for a few moments, and then a new possibility occurred to her. "I don't suppose you know anything else about Sarita's family."

"You kiddin'? Sweetie, I've lived all my life in this town of eleven-hundred people. I know just about everything about everybody, and unfortunately, they know the same about me."

"Okay, what about Sarita's mother?"

"Carmen? Good kid. Of course, I say *kid* but she's probably almost thirty old by now. She's married to the guy who runs the insurance company about two blocks in that direction." He pointed. "Why do you ask?"

"I'm not sure. Just grasping at straws, mostly. Any other Saritas in the family tree?"

"Hmmm. You know, I think Carmen's great-grandma may have had that name, but everybody always called her Grammy Torres, so I might be wrong."

Emily leaned toward him, her shoulder harness tightening against her. All other thoughts had fled. Suddenly this was all that mattered. "Sarita's great-great-grandmother was also named Sarita?"

"Uh, maybe. I don't know. Like I said, as long as I ever knew her, everybody around town just called her Grammy Torres. She passed away...oh, it must be almost twenty years ago. Maybe more. Why?"

Emily wasn't prone to hunches. But she felt one now, so powerful that it made her short of breath. "I need to speak with Carmen."

"I reckon she's at work. She helps out over at the daycare on the west side of town."

"Take me there, *now*."

"You sure?"

"I'll double your daily rate."

"What on earth for?"

"Goddammit, Tunny, *drive*."

Tunny cranked the wheel in a hard left-hand turn, then pushed the gas pedal to the floor.

Chapter Thirty-Two

Kids Korner Daycare stood in the shadow of the city water tower. Inside the low fence was a battleground for make-believe, with toys strewn across the trampled grass like fallen soldiers. The jungle gym, made of old tires and steel pipe, was designed to look like a pirate's ship. The merry-go-round was brightly painted but slightly angled from too many years of hard play.

Tunny pulled in between two minivans.

"Can you introduce me to Carmen?" Emily asked.

"Are you goin' to tell me what this is all about?"

"I don't have it all sorted out yet. Ask me again tomorrow."

"Count on it." He got out, and Emily followed him through the gate.

They were halfway up the walk when the front door burst open, admitting half a dozen cannonballs in disguise as three-year-olds. They blew across the yard with whoops and laughter, glad to be under the sun. Walking out behind them were two women, one with gray streaks in her hair and the other much younger.

"That's her there on the right," Tunny said. He waved as they approached, removing his hat as the four of them converged on the sidewalk in the middle of the suddenly rambunctious yard.

"Why, Paul Tunny," the older woman said. "I

haven't seen you in a raccoon's age."

"Howdy, ma'am."

"No reason to go all 'ma'am' on me, unless you're here asking for a favor."

"That's not far from the truth, I reckon."

"Oh?"

He looked at Carmen. "Actually, Mrs. Thomas, it's *you* we're here to see. This here is my friend Emily. She's from New Jersey. She doin' research—historical stuff, I guess you'd say."

Emily took that as her cue. She introduced herself and extended her hand, glad to find that it wasn't trembling in anticipation. Was she closing in on clues to Sarita's past? "It's a pleasure to meet you. It's Carmen, isn't it?"

"That's correct. Uh, what can I do to help you?"

"I know this is unexpected, and it may sound a little strange...or a *lot* strange, now that I mention it. But..." She stalled, unsure of how to proceed. She was going to sound like a lunatic no matter how it came out, so she figured she might as well just say it. "Are you related to anyone named Sarita?"

Now Carmen looked worried. "My daughter? Is something wrong—"

"No, not at all. It's not your daughter. I'm sorry, I didn't mean to frighten you. I'm sure your daughter's fine. I mean, is there maybe a grandmother..."

"Grammy Torres?"

"Honestly I'm not sure. What was her full name?"

"Sarita Torres. Why?"

Emily reminded herself to take this slowly, lest she come across as not only crazy but dangerous. With stalkers so prevalent in the media these days, you could never be too careful. "Would you mind if I talk to you about her? I'm a doctoral candidate conducting research on certain historical aspects of this region's early twentieth-century immigrants, and I think Sarita Torres may be an important part of that investigation."

"Seriously? Wow. I never thought anyone in the family did anything worth mentioning. But sure, I'd love to help."

"You have a few minutes? I don't want to be interrupting you at work."

"No, it's okay." She glanced at the older woman, who nodded. "I'm just playing lifeguard right now," Carmen said. "We can talk while I keep an eye on these rug rats."

"Sounds good. Tunny?"

"I'll be fine. You two take your time."

Carmen led her to the fence. She shaded her eyes with her hand and gave the playground a thorough inspection. "Looks like Cody isn't throwing sand in anyone's eyes today, so we're already making improvements over yesterday."

Emily wanted to dive into the discussion but held herself in check. She also wanted Mason here at her side, but her call had gone straight to voice mail.

"So what would you like to know about Grammy Torres?"

"A lot of things, if that's okay."

"Sure, but why her? I wasn't aware that she'd ever done anything worth mentioning, other than raising a family and being kind of locally famous for her blueberry muffins. When she passed, she was the oldest living person in the county, and that got a mention in the paper."

"Her name came up in my research. I'm just following all the leads. Your daughter is named after her?"

"Yep. Grammy died when I was eleven. It hit me kind of hard. She'd lived right next door, and we were always over there, running around just like these kids right here, chasing her chickens. I thought it would be nice to pass the name on, and my husband really liked it. Our next-best option was to name her Mandy, after Jason's mom, but I wasn't really hot on that one."

"You said she was very old when she died?"

"Ninety-nine, almost to the day. She got along well, considering. She had arthritis in just about every joint, but she did okay."

"And she was your *great*-grandmother?"

"That's right."

"Paternal?"

"Nope, she was from my mom's side. My mother passed four years ago. Breast cancer."

"I'm sorry." Emily wanted to say more. *I'm sorry* didn't seem like enough when it was somebody's mother you were talking about.

"Thanks. That was hard, too. It never gets any easier, does it?"

Emily shifted her weight from one foot to the other. She wanted to know everything at once, but the big question involved Carmen's great-grandfather. Had he been a shepherd in his youth?

"Play nice, Dillon!" Carmen called across the yard. "There's room on there for everyone!"

"So…your great-grandmother married a man by the last name of Torres?"

"What? No, that's her maiden name. Grammy

never married."

"She didn't?"

Carmen shook her head. "I guess it was probably seen as risqué back then, but Grammy had her only child—my grandma—out of wedlock."

Emily ran this through her mind. If Grammy Torres was the same Sarita referenced in the shepherd's notes, then why hadn't they married? Emily wanted a happy ending, but if Carmen was right, then she might be in for tragedy. She wasn't sure if she should keep asking questions or leave well enough alone.

"Is that not what you wanted to hear?" Carmen asked.

"Sorry, it's not that. Sometimes what you uncover in your research surprises you. Do you know anything about the father of her baby—your great-grandfather?"

"My mom never knew him, and neither did my grandma. I don't think Grammy ever talked about him."

"What about...his name? Do you know his name?"

Again Carmen shook her head.

"You don't know?"

"It never came up."

And so the shepherd remains a mystery. Emily needed more information. Instinct told her that she'd found the right Sarita. Now all that remained was to fill in the empty spaces. And there were a lot of them. "Is there anyone, a relative or someone, who might know something about him?"

"I doubt it. Grandma was an only child."

"What about your grandma's birth certificate? It should list the names of her parents on it."

"I probably have it around somewhere...maybe. Things like that tend to fall through the cracks. If you want to know the truth, I threw away a lot of my mother's business and bank records after she passed, and most of grandma's paperwork was in there, too. There really wasn't any need to keep it. But I can check when I get home tonight. There's a box in the back closet that might be what you're looking for. Most of the stuff in there was Mom's, but I think I have a few things of Grammy's in there, as well."

"Would you mind?"

"Not at all. It's just sitting back there. I haven't touched it in many years. What's this research about, anyway?"

"Love."

Carmen looked away from the children. "Love?"

Emily hadn't meant to say it. It just came out. But standing here on this playground near a merry-go-round that squeaked with every revolution, she decided that her thesis had changed. Now there was only one topic that mattered. "I think your Grammy Torres might have had an incredible love affair, but I can't prove it. You're here today because of that love."

"That's not something you hear every day."

"I know that sounds really off the wall but—"

"No, it sounds nice."

"I might be wrong. Maybe I'm just making up the details based on sketchy evidence. That could very well turn out to be true. But I won't know for certain until I learn everything about your great-grandmother than I can. And I need your help to do it."

"Okay, you've got it." She seemed to be weighing something in her mind, then apparently came to a decision. "You want to see a picture of her when she was young?"

Emily felt herself drawing closer to the center of the shepherd's story. "Very much so."

"Give me twenty minutes. I'll take an early lunch."

"Are you sure? I can come back at a better time. I don't want to inconvenience you."

"No inconvenience. Just promise that you'll let me know any juicy details you uncover."

Emily drew an X across her chest with the tip of one finger. "Cross my heart."

****

Mason parked the company truck in front of his house and stared at his phone. He didn't want to tell her that her campsite was gone. They'd harvested the last tree in the quadrant. Some of those specimens had been growing since the shepherd's time, over a hundred years ago. Sure, they'd replant many of the areas—the company would take a public beating if it didn't maintain some kind of sustainable environmental policy—but what was gone would never come back.

"Coward," he said to himself, turning the phone over in his hands. Emily was probably still at the library, back aching from being bent over old newsprint all day. He hoped she didn't feel as sullen as he did.

On Monday he planned to hand in his resignation. That should have thrilled him. Instead it only compounded his anxiety. Where would they go from here? Had it been only the aspens that held them together? Would their love be able to thrive without the thrill of a wilderness mystery between them?

And more practically speaking, what the hell was he going to do to pay the bills? "Sell my body on the street corner," he said with a grin.

He dialed her number and waited for her to pick

up. She didn't answer by the third ring. Of course, if she were in the library, she'd probably silenced her phone—

She picked up. "Hey, you."

The simple sound of her voice eased much of his discontent. That made it a bit easier to tell her the truth: "I cut down our tree today."

"You're forgiven."

"You know the one. We, uh, were kind of naked behind it."

"I said you're forgiven."

"So easily?"

"I found Sarita."

Mason almost lost his grip on the phone. "Come again?"

"It's been quite a day. But I found her. I followed the family tree."

"Explain."

"She has relatives. Descendants. They still live here in Rockerton."

"Who?"

"A woman named Carmen Thomas."

"Carmen Thomas?" He sorted through his mental database. Rockerton was no metropolis, with barely more than a thousand residents, and he'd lived here long enough to be at least dimly familiar with most of the family names. "She's married to the insurance agent, right?"

"Correct. Jason and Carmen Thomas. They have a little girl, Sarita's great-great granddaughter. And her namesake. I'm at their house right now. It's on the corner of Sheridan and Pine."

"So...you figured everything out?"

"Not exactly, but we're a lot closer than we were this morning. Now I have a question for you."

"Go ahead."

"You want to see what Sarita looked like back then?"

"Seriously?"

"Get your ass over here, sailor." She hung up.

Mason dropped the phone onto the seat and cranked the key. He hit the gas hard enough that the back tires threw up plumes of dirt. He drove the mile into town faster than he ever had, hit Pine Avenue, and turned right. The depth of his curiosity surprised him.

Maybe this was how the archaeologists felt when they found a tablet buried in the sand, a chapter of an ancient story that hadn't been told in ages. And best of all was the fact that he was sharing this discovery with the most dynamic woman he'd ever known. But like the tale of Sarita and the shepherd, that of Mason and Emily still had much to be revealed.

He saw Tunny sitting in the cab of his truck, hat pulled over his eyes. Mason parked behind him, got out, and then looked down at himself. Sawdust filled the creases of his jeans, and his boots looked like they'd been through the deltas of Vietnam. He'd planned on showering and changing before seeing Emily tonight. She was classy and deserved someone without sweat stains on his shirt.

He sighed, then moved to Tunny's truck and knocked on the glass.

Tunny sat up and unrolled the window. "Hey there, Mace. Your lady friend's inside, diggin' through the attic or somethin'."

"Thanks."

"What's she lookin' for, anyway?"

"The secret."

"The secret of what?"

"Everything."

"Damn. Sounds ambitious."

"More than you know. You don't need to hang around. I can give her a ride when she's done."

"You're the boss. Tell her to give me a holler the next time she needs me."

"Will do." Mason didn't watch him leave. He headed for the house and rang the bell.

While he waited, he wondered where they'd live. She needed to return to the East Coast to finish her academic work. Would he go with her? Was there a market in the big city for handmade furniture? He supposed there was. And custom carpentry probably commanded higher prices than it did in Colorado. But would he be able to function in that environment? Between the traffic and the skyscrapers, would he be able to breathe?

The door opened, revealing a woman whom he vaguely recognized. "You must be Mason."

"Carmen Thomas?"

"Come on in. Emily's in the kitchen with my great-grandmother. So to speak."

Mason wiped his boots on the mat, then followed Carmen through her modest living room to the kitchen.

Emily sat behind a semicircle of papers and yellowed envelopes. She stood up as soon as she saw him, taking his hands in hers. "You know how to keep a girl waiting."

"I drove like the proverbial bat out of you-know-where."

"And that was still too slow. Sit down."

He loved seeing her this way, filled with such enthusiasm. He sat as instructed.

Carmen offered him a glass of tea. "Can I get you anything? Emily, a refill?"

Emily declined, but Mason couldn't resist. With tree-cutting behind him—perhaps forever—nothing sounded better than iced tea. It made for just as fine a celebration as champagne.

"Just yell if you need anything," Carmen said, and left them alone with the only remnants of her great-grandmother that remained.

"So what do you have?" Mason asked.

"Close your eyes."

He did so without question or hesitation.

"Okay, behold Sarita Torres."

He opened his eyes.

The woman looking back at him from the small black-and-white photograph was younger than he'd imagined, with dusky Spanish skin and a beauty as fragile as porcelain. She smiled only faintly, as if uncertain of the camera even though she looked perfectly comfortable in front of it. Her dimpled chin was a heart breaker, for sure, and Mason immediately sympathized with the shepherd, whoever he was. A man would've had to be carved from wood not to fall for that dimple.

He didn't know what to say. "She's…"

"Stunning?"

"Not quite. But she probably was in real life."

"I agree."

"How do you know it's her?"

"Faith." She looked at the picture. "Maybe it's not

the same Sarita. But the time line fits."

"So what about the shepherd?"

"That's the bad part. Nobody knows anything about him."

"Not even his name?"

"Sarita was pregnant but wasn't married or even engaged. Back then, this was a serious taboo. Depending on the specific culture, it might have even made her a pariah. That was why she never talked about it. And the father of her child was never around. I get the feeling that her relationship with him was short-lived."

"I don't buy it. This wasn't just a fling. Guys who have flings don't go around hiding messages in metal tubes and banging them into trees. Something must have happened to him."

"Like what?"

"I don't know. Maybe Sarita's dad was so upset about her pregnancy that he hunted down the culprit and killed him with the family shotgun. She never married anyone?"

"Never. An eternal spinster."

"Interesting. What else do you have?"

"Not much. Sarita lived in Rockerton before the town was incorporated. She never had a birth certificate. It was still a little bit like the Wild West out here back then. As far as anyone knows, she never graduated high school. But she made a mean batch of blueberry muffins. I have several pictures here of when she was older."

"No, I don't want to see them."

"She was a very happy and loving grandma."

"I'm sure she was. But if it's all the same, I'll keep

the shepherd's girl in mind." He took the faded picture from her and studied it again. It was easy to see how a man could lose his mind for a woman like this. Maybe she wouldn't go on to earn a diploma, but the charm and spirit she carried were unmistakable. Yet she hadn't married. Which meant that the shepherd had been her greatest love, never to be replaced. Why, then, had he left her? Or had she left him?

"I need to know what happened to him," he said.

"How do we find out? It's my guess that Sarita never told anyone who the father was, maybe to protect him, maybe to protect herself. Carmen told me that her great-grandma was a first-generation American. Her parents were immigrant farmers from Spain. Sarita was deeply Catholic, living in a very rural place in a very conservative time so talking about the father of her illegitimate child probably wasn't very high on her list of priorities."

"I still need to know."

"But *how?*"

"This is everything?"

"Yes, this box, that's all. I have plenty of things from her later years, but that doesn't help us very much. What we're looking for is what transpired during a time in her life that's been blanked out."

"He didn't just go away. Not from her. Something happened to him."

"Is this turning into a conspiracy theory?"

"It might. Reel me back in if I start talking about UFO abductions."

"Will do."

Carmen stepped back into the kitchen. "How's it going in here?"

"I think we're about finished," Emily said, neatly returning the documents to the box.

Mason held up the photo. "May we take a picture of this? So we have a copy?"

"Sure. I'm glad to help."

They finished cleaning up after themselves and said goodbye to Carmen at the door, promising to return the original picture by tomorrow.

"No need to hurry," she assured them. "Oh, and if you're interested, Grammy is buried in the cemetery north of town. Her marker isn't anything fancy. We wanted to do more, but she insisted on exactly what it should say and how it should look."

"That's a good idea," Mason said immediately, grasping at whatever might lead them to the next clue. "I think we'll definitely check it out. Thanks."

"No problem. You two come back anytime. It's nice to think that Grammy was somebody worth researching. I was only a kid when she died, but I loved her a lot."

"You're not the only one," Mason said, and left her with that cryptic line.

Emily took his hand as they made their way to his truck. "So we're off to the cemetery?"

"Wild horses."

"I'm sorry?"

"They couldn't keep me away."

"Don't be upset if this doesn't lead anywhere. Okay?"

It wasn't okay. Mason squeezed her hand but said nothing.

"Fine," Emily said. "Then let's go spend some quality time in a graveyard."

Chapter Thirty-Three

Walnut Ridge Cemetery wasn't situated on a ridge at all, and there were no walnut trees around, at least none that Emily could see. A chain-link fence surrounded the carefully tended grounds. The most prominent building was a red-brick caretaker's shed with Indian laurels planted in neat rows around it. As she and Mason walked quietly through the gate, Emily got the same feeling she always got when visiting these places: aloneness.

She rested her hand in the crook of his elbow."I'm glad you're here."

"Where else would I be?"

"Home, maybe. If you hadn't been driving down the hill at that precise moment, you wouldn't be here right now. We never would've met."

"Kismet."

"You think?"

"I don't know. I've never been one to put much stock in the idea of destiny. My grandfather once said that nothing is written until a man takes up his own brush and writes it on the sky."

Emily let that image move through her. Again she realized how much the modern world was missing when it failed to listen to the wisdom of its elders.

"We should've asked Carmen the location of Sarita's grave marker," Mason said.

"There aren't that many. You take that side of the path. I'll take this one."

They separated, veering off to study the stones one at a time. Every so often, Emily looked up just to get her eyes on him again. Was he serious about quitting his job? Would he follow her when she flew back home? Or would this weekend be the end? Emily hoped their story wasn't tied so completely to that of Sarita and her lover that their failure to resolve the latter would mean trouble for the former. She'd never wanted a man like this. Or anything else, for that matter.

She reminded herself to get back to work.

The rows continued, one after the next. She played her eyes over the names, people she'd never met, lives she'd never known. Judging by the dates, most had lived well into their seventies or eighties, though a few had been taken early, and these were the ones that intrigued her. A woman dead at twenty-four. A child called home at twelve. Emily had never been one to fantasize about the glamour of dying young, but now that she was considering these prematurely deceased strangers, perhaps their lives had been brighter and bolder because they'd been cut so short.

She moved faster.

Of course she should've had the foresight to ask Carmen about the general location of her great-grandmother's stone. But she hadn't thought that far ahead. The cemetery wasn't that large, so surely they'd eventually find it if they—

"I've got her!"

Emily jogged toward him, and then turned her jog into a run. She chose a path that didn't take her directly across the plots; though she was eager to see what he'd found, she gave the dead the respect they deserved. When she reached him, he was on his knees beside it, a flat gray slab almost flush with the grass.

SARITA ANA TORRES
YOU ARE MY SHEPHERD. I SHALL NOT
WANT.

Below this inscription were the dates of her birth and death. She'd lived ninety-eight years and three-hundred and sixty-four days.

"So here she is." Emily couldn't help but reach out and touch the stone. "We found her."

"Looks like we did."

Emily traced the woman's name with her finger, then moved to the Bible verse beneath. She read again, then frowned. "Is this right?"

"What do you mean?"

"This piece of scripture."

"It's the twenty-third psalm, isn't it?"

"Is it?"

"Sure. It's common to read it at funerals. It's comforting."

"But how does it go, exactly?" She knew the answer, but she asked anyway.

"I'm no Bible scholar," Mason admitted, "but I think it goes, 'The Lord is my shepherd, I shall not want.'"

"Exactly. And that's not what this says."

Mason read it again. "You're right. *You are my shepherd*. She's not talking to God here, is she?"

She seized Mason's hand. "She's talking about *him*. Her shepherd."

"Maybe."

"Maybe nothing. Carmen said they made this

marker exactly how her great-grandmother wanted it. This is how she wanted the verse to read. *You are my shepherd.* She's talking directly to *him*."

Mason shifted in the grass, rocking back and resting his arms on his knees.

"You know it's true," Emily said.

"Could be."

"What they had together was the real thing. That's why she never found anyone else after he was gone."

"That's the problem. Where did he go?"

Emily sighed and sat beside him, close enough that their elbows touched. "I'm sure if we did a little more digging, we could find out. I haven't been through all the newspapers at the library yet, and though they didn't keep accurate census records back then—"

"Some mysteries are like the clouds. They move across the sky, and then they're gone."

"Spoken like a true Indian."

Mason smiled. "What would you say if I offered to make you dinner?"

"I'd say you need a shower first."

"I guess that could be arranged. But they say one of the best ways to conserve water is to shower in twos."

Emily raised an eyebrow. "Is that what they say?"

"They do."

"Who are 'they' anyway?"

He kissed her. "I meant *me*."

"That's what I thought." She kissed him back.

****

With a hand on either side of the sink, Mason studied his reflection.

Was that man brave enough to remake his life with this woman?

"Yes."

It wasn't a matter of bravery. Nothing in this town kept him here. He could sell the cabin to a yuppie from Golden or an import from L.A. His only valuable possessions were the pieces of furniture he'd made himself and his tools. He had no relatives begging him to stay. So he'd already made his decision. In fact, he'd made it days ago. Yet if that were the case and he was dreaming of buying a house with a view of the Atlantic, then why was he standing here debating it with himself?

"The damn shepherd," he said.

He and Emily had eaten dinner while night fell outside the windows. They'd laughed like they'd known each other for years, then she reclined against his chest as they watched an old Rock Hudson movie on Mason's ten-year-old TV. They hadn't talked at all of Sarita and what leaving her would mean. But Mason's curiosity had transformed. Finding the answers to the shepherd's riddle had become a borderline obsession.

"Are you hiding in there?" Emily called through the bathroom door.

"Yes, you terrify me!" he yelled back.

"I'm about to do a lot more than that to you."

Mason smiled to himself. She was almost too good to believe. He'd waited all his life to find someone like her, and when she appeared, she was nothing like what he'd expected. No, it wasn't about bravery. He'd fight an army for her. It was simply about the shepherd and finding out *what happened next*.

"It's awfully lonely out here!"

He stepped away from the mirror and left the

bathroom, happy to end her solitude.

As he slid in beside her, she said, "I was starting to wonder if I'd been stood up."

"I was thinking about sleeping on the couch."

"Oh, is that so?"

"You snore."

She punched him. "I do no such thing!"

"And you take up too much of the bed."

"Maybe, but at least I'm warm."

He moved his hand down her leg. "True." He kissed her gently. "Tomorrow's Saturday."

"Uh-huh."

"Do you want to take a field trip?"

"Where to?"

"The hill. Back up where the trees used to be."

"What for?"

"I want to walk where he walked one last time."

"Why?"

"Maybe his ghost is up there, hanging around."

"Sounds good. But let's worry about that tomorrow."

"You're right. It's best if we just roll over and get some sleep."

She pinched him.

"Ouch!"

"Don't make me use my kung-fu on you," she said, "because I will if you don't watch out."

"Come here." He pulled her on top of him and— for the next hour, at least—thought no more of the shepherd.

Chapter Thirty-Four

.The next morning, Emily visited the woods for what she suspected would be the last time. The sun in the east promised a glorious day, as warm as any she'd felt since embarking on her quest here in Colorado. They'd parked just off the logging track, and as Mason retrieved their lunch from the cooler, Emily stood with her face in the warmth of a new day.

And a new life, she thought.

She'd reinvented herself once already, a decade ago when she'd left behind her listless lifestyle and enrolled in school. And this weekend? Another incarnation of Emily Radsco was being born, this one entirely new.

"Ready?" Mason asked.

Emily took his hand, and together they made their way to the remains of her campsite.

White stumps stood where trees had once been. The entire area had been harvested, the lumber loaded onto trucks and hauled away. Small limbs and a thousand drying leaves carpeted the ground. Jagged sticks lay here and there, and there was no sign of wildlife. It looked as if a bomb had been detonated.

"My God," Emily whispered.

"If it's any consolation, and I know it's not, the company will replant this area next season. That's part of the deal."

"I know. But looking at it is still…strange. All the trees we're been examining for dendroglyphs…"

"Let's walk."

They left the ravaged acres behind and headed downhill into the standing forest. Emily felt better as soon as they entered the tree line, which was odd, since she'd been born a city girl and had no business being so comfortable in the wild. But the serenity of the place was something she couldn't deny. Maybe after she completed her doctorate—*if* she completed her doctorate—the two of them could move someplace where trees still mattered.

They walked for half an hour, the sunlight finding them through the boughs. Emily didn't recognize this part of the wood; she hadn't traveled this far down the slope until now. As they went, they spoke tentatively of their plans beyond this weekend. Emily was excited by the prospect of sharing her small apartment with him, but at the same time she was terrified. Cohabitation was not a thing to be taken lightly. There were certain mornings when she could hardly stand to live with herself. How hard would it be living with a man?

"Easy," she said, holding his hand.

"Easy what?"

"That's how all of this seems. So…effortless."

"I'm a fairly low-maintenance guy."

"I noticed."

"Low-maintenance and scared to death."

"Scared of what? Me?"

"Scared I'm going to be the proverbial round peg trying to fit into the square hole of the East Coast."

"Handmade furniture sells for a ton in the city. You'll love it."

"Maybe."

"Besides, who said we had to stay there for the rest of our lives? I'm starting to get fond of being surrounded by trees. What do you say we don't worry about it right now? It just makes me nervous. And I eat when I'm nervous, so unless you have some chocolate ice cream in that lunch bag of yours, we should change the subject."

"Agreed. There's a little clearing over there. How does that look?"

They made their way into the glen. A series of gray-white rocks thrust up from the ground in a horseshoe pattern. Mason sat down and leaned his back against one, spinning the cap from a bottle of water.

Emily sat in front of him, accepting the bottle when he offered it. She asked him a dozen questions about things important and insignificant, just to hear him talk. He allowed himself to be subjected to this lighthearted interrogation for twenty minutes before turning the tables on her, which she enjoyed more than she let on.

"How did you hear about the markings on the trees, anyway?" he asked.

"Boredom, actually."

"What do you mean?"

"About a week before I completed my master's thesis, I was reading random junk online, just wasting time because I was so sick of writing. I came across a brief mention of a dendroglyph that had been found in Wyoming. I'd never heard the term before then, so I looked it up. I was hooked from that point on. A few months later I came across a reference to a similar mark that a hiker had seen here in Colorado."

"And the rest is history."

"And I met you, and *then* the rest is history."

"I'm crazy for you," he said. "You know that, don't you?"

Emily's smile wasn't sufficient to express the emotion that welled up within her.

He placed the nearly emptied water bottle on a rock, turning its cap in his fingers. "I think about you even when I don't want to be thinking about you. I feel like all the years since I left Arizona, I've just been waiting for you to show up."

She lunged toward him and wrapped her arms around his neck. "*Thank you.*"

He hugged her and stroked her hair. "I'm soon going to be unemployed, you know."

"I don't care."

"I'm allergic to cats."

"I don't own a cat."

"I tend to walk around the house naked."

"I look forward to it."

He rocked her. "Then maybe all of this will work out, after all."

Emily just held on and enjoyed the feeling of him, but then she noticed something about the rocks.

Mason must have felt her stiffen. "What's wrong? What did I say?"

"Nothing it's just..." She pulled back from him, her eyes never leaving the white stones. They were arranged in a kind of half-circle, a natural formation that had been exposed when the surrounding soil was rubbed away by wind and rain.

"Emily?" He turned to followed her gaze. "What is it? What do you see?"

On her knees, she moved from one rock to the

next, playing her hands over them.

"You're kind of freaking me out here," Mason said as he got to his feet. "What's the matter?"

"I'm not sure." The rock formation looked familiar, which was of course impossible, as she'd never been here before. And that's what so excited her. Something important was happening, and if she could...just...

She stopped, her breath caught in her throat.

Mason reached for her, then withdrew, as if afraid to touch her.

"Mason?"

"I'm right here."

"What did the note say?"

"Note?"

"The shepherd's message. The second one."

"Uh, something about...when the moon comes up, Sarita was supposed to meet him."

"Meet him where?"

"At the...it was a funny phrase—the hill teeth smile."

Emily pointed to the curve of jagged white stones. "What do these look like to you?"

Mason put his hands on his hips and studied the scene. "Are you thinking this is it?"

"Use your imagination. You're a simple sheep-herder from a hundred years ago. You look at this configuration of exposed rock. What does it look like?"

"Like the letter U."

"Or?"

"Or...maybe like teeth?"

"That's right." The thrill of the chase gave her goosebumps. "Maybe like teeth."

"But there's nothing here but a patch of grass."

"A lot of time has passed since then," Emily reminded him. She knelt in the center of the half-ring of stones and put both hands in the grass, where she suspected something might be buried below. "You were right about the cave."

Mason squatted beside her. "There *is* no cave. Hey, look at me." He took her hands. "I was wrong when I said I was crazy about you."

"You're changing your mind?"

"Got that right. I'm not crazy about you. I'm in love with you."

Emily inhaled deeply of that, wanting to capture it, hold it, keep it safe. She'd never heard any words that had ever had such a lightening effect on her. She felt as if she might float away. But then she thought of the shepherd, and she grounded herself again.

"That means almost everything to me," she said. "And I suspect it will change my life from this point forward. It already has. But at this moment, right now, I don't need your love."

She squeezed his hands. "I need a shovel."

Chapter Thirty-Five

She waited half an hour for Mason to return. He had hiked back to the truck and made the short drive home. He would come back armed with proper digging gear.

In the meantime, Emily paced and considered what he'd said.

I'm in love with you.

Had it happened so fast? She'd met him only ten days ago. *Ten.* Was it possible to create the foundation of a lasting relationship in that amount of time? Was it possible in such a short span to want a man so badly and be wanted by him in return that nothing else mattered?

Well, *almost* nothing else. She kicked at the grass, wondering what it concealed.

She wouldn't have made it this far without him. Mason was more than her lover. He was her partner in this investigation, and had he not entered her life, she wouldn't be standing here now, impatiently waiting to discover what was buried below. Her personal and professional lives had converged, with Mason at the center of both.

"Honey, I'm home!" he shouted through the trees.

She smiled. "Over here, hero."

He appeared suddenly, a long-handled spade over each shoulder and a rucksack on his back. "Glad to see you weren't eaten by a bear while I was gone."

"I fought several of them off. It's probably best you missed the violence."

"Yeah, I have a faint heart." He kissed her, then positioned his dual shovels like ski poles. "Choose your weapon, my lady."

Emily gladly did so, though her expertise with such a tool was rather limited. "I want to say up front that I am by no means a veteran digger."

"Have you ever planted vegetables?"

"I can't even keep houseplants alive, much less anything edible."

He laughed that daring laugh of his. "I'll teach you. Next summer we'll plant squash."

"Then next summer we're going to need a yard. I live in an apartment."

He shrugged to say it would all work out as Sky Father intended, and Emily happily believed him.

He gave her some gloves, and they got to work.

Emily learned quickly the most fundamental fact about digging a hole: it looked much easier in the movies. But in real life, holes didn't happen quickly, as least not ones of significant depth. She observed Mason's form and emulated it, breaking it down into three parts. First she pushed the shovel's pointed end an inch into the black soil. Then she used her foot to bring her weight down on the thing, driving the blade as deep as she could. When she encountered a particularly resistant patch of earth, she hopped onto the shovel and bounced twice, like a woman on a pogo stick. Mason grinned and said he liked her style.

"You know," he said, "I suppose technically we're not supposed to be digging here."

Emily heaved another load of dirt onto the growing mound behind her. "Tunny told me that it was okay to camp out here."

"Camp, yes. Dig a tunnel to mainland China, maybe not."

"Okay, so if we strike oil, it belongs to somebody else. I can live with that."

They kept working.

After a while Mason said, "I didn't mean to lay anything heavy on you, by the way. I don't usually go around telling women I love them. If that made you uncomfortable—"

"Shut up and dig."

"Yes, ma'am."

Emily smiled to herself. If Mason knew the truth, he might drop his shovel and run. Not only was she comfortable with his feelings for her, she was already mentally rearranging her closet to accommodate his clothes. Sometimes you took your time with these things, and sometimes you just flew with it as fast as you could.

An hour passed.

They shifted positions, trying different locations within the half-ring of white stones.

Emily looked up only when Mason peeled his T-shirt off. Her own shoveling suffered a bit after that, as she too frequently stole glances at him as he worked. The physical attraction was nice. Falling for someone's soul was, of course, the best option, but there was nothing wrong with lusting after their body at the same time. She'd spent so long cloistered in the stale halls of the university that she'd almost forgotten how to—

"I found something."

She turned immediately. "What is it?"

"A hollow space." He sank down and worked his hand into the hole he'd encountered.

Emily let her shovel fall and joined him. "Let me see."

He removed his hand so she could get a look.

"Here, try this." He handed her a flashlight from his rucksack.

She stabbed the beam into the hole. "I think it might be a tunnel." She looked up, the excitement of discovery coursing through her. "We found it."

"We *might* have found it. Let's see if I can dig it out without collapsing it."

She got out of the way, and Mason carefully used the shovel blade to widen the hole, removing any dirt that fell into it. Sweat had formed along his neckline and across the back of his shoulders. Twenty minutes later, he'd cleared a passage about two feet wide. Emily aimed the flashlight into it, revealing a shallow cavity about ten feet back.

"It's a cave," she said, hardly believing it herself. "Mason, *it's a cave*."

He peered into it, following the light. "There's something in there."

"What is it?"

"I guess there's only one way to find out." He motioned for her to proceed. "Ladies first. Unless you want me to lead the way and check for snakes."

"I'll take my chances." She got down on her hands and knees and inhaled the scent of moist soil. This was it, the place where Sarita and her lover had met. Over one hundred years ago, they'd visited this very spot. And now...and now Emily was about to explore it.

She crawled into the cave.

****

Of Sarita Torres and the man she loved, only a single object remained. Everything else lay in ruin. What might have been a basket was now bits of crumbled, hardened straw. A blanket spread across the cave floor was nothing but an outline of flakes and fibers, mostly consumed by the ground and the things that lived there. Tiny shards of glass flickered like diamonds in the flashlight beam. If that glass had once represented a lantern or bottle, Emily would never know.

But the chest was mostly intact.

It was smaller than a steamer trunk but stronger. Made of metal, the box was perhaps twenty inches long and half as deep. Rust claimed most of it. Only the buckles remained of the leather straps that had once secured the container, and the walls had softened and bulged with age. But otherwise it was whole.

Emily said nothing. Breaking the silence would've seemed like sacrilege.

Mason nodded toward the chest. She heard his mental message: *Go ahead.*

Scholars had proper ways of opening archeological and historical artifacts. There was an accepted and time-honored methodology to these things, and Emily would certainly be violating a number of rules if she simply put her hand to the thing and threw it open. At the very least, she needed to be photographing everything as she examined it, but she wasn't about to worry over her phone. Not now.

Mason gave the light a shake. *What are you waiting for?*

His thoughts were Emily's own. She could wait no longer. After a bit of prying with Mason's chisel, she lifted the lid.

Two items rested inside the metal coffer. The first was a flower, dried to the point of such fragility that Emily knew it would disintegrate at a touch. She left it there and removed the second object—a book. Its covers were ceramic slats, bound by wire at the spine. The loose folio pages within were written in a combination of Spanish and English.

Mason trained the light on the writing.

Emily read Sarita's words aloud. "'Gone a fortnight now you are, and I long to be with you, across the land and sea.'"

"Sarita wrote that?" Mason asked.

"Yes."

"Is this her diary?"

"Something like that. There are letters here, and personal notes, and…" She forced herself to take several steady breaths. "This is *everything*."

"So we were right? The two of them really did meet here?"

"Seems that way."

"Keep reading already. I'm dying here."

Emily scanned for the next passage written in English. "'Are you even today fighting, my love? Are you raising your saber against the very country you call home?'"

"What does that mean? Who was he fighting?"

"I'm not sure." She moved through the pages until she found more. "'I have never known the white shores of your Cuba, but I hope one day to see them with you.'"

"Cuba?"

Emily's mind bounded back through her undergrad years, searching for the facts. "World history was never my strong suit, but if the shepherd was off fighting in Cuba, then I think Sarita must be talking about...the Spanish-American War."

"The shepherd was a soldier?"

"Maybe not at first. But then the war started, and he probably volunteered. And she uses the phrase *your Cuba*, which means he was either Cuban or supported their cause." She imagined him traveling overland and then boarding a ship to his native country, leaving behind the baby he wouldn't live to hold. "That explains why his daughter never knew him."

"He died over there."

"He did."

"So Sarita waited for him, but he never came back. And she never loved another."

Emily nodded. "And after he was gone, Sarita returned to this cave and put her journal and a flower in this metal box, so that no one would ever know the truth."

"Okay, but why? Why wouldn't she want anyone to know?"

Emily thought the best way to find out was to keep reading. "'They will say you made the wrong decision, that you chose poorly when you took up arms, or even that you were a traitor to this nation we both so dearly love.'" She looked up. "The shepherd fought for the other side."

Mason shook his head in apparent disbelief. "Incredible. But I guess it makes sense, though. He was either Cuban or a Spaniard himself. He went to help his people, maybe his own mother and father. And that meant fighting against U.S. troops."

"Which was one more reason that Sarita would've been reluctant to tell anyone about him. They would have alienated her and her baby." Now that the secrets were finally turning over and revealing themselves, Emily was eager for more. She dove back into the book, drawing her finger down the fragile page. "'I shall wait for you, like the snow-covered mountain awaits the spring. Until then, I remain your Sarita, and you are forever my—'"

"Wait." Mason moved the light so that it no longer illuminated the page. "I don't think I want to know his name."

"Why not?"

"It's just…I don't know. I guess I don't want to the mystery to be over."

"Naming him doesn't make it over."

"Doesn't it? Even without translating the Spanish portion of these letters, I already know enough of the story to be satisfied, at least for now. Spain puts out a call for patriots to protect its interests in Cuba, and Sarita's lover responds, for whatever reason. He died over there and never returned to her. I don't need to know any more about his motivations or his family tree. And before you say it, yes, I realize that all of this information will eventually come out, and you'll publish it as part of your dissertation and maybe get famous because of it. But that's for tomorrow."

"You're such a romantic."

"Guilty as charged."

They kissed, there in the darkness of a cave that had been closed for a century or more, and Emily felt her body responding. Overcome with the exhilaration of unearthing Sarita's past, she longed to celebrate in this man's embrace.

Mason suddenly broke the kiss. "Hold on."

"What? What's wrong?"

"Forget all that stuff I just said. I can't stand it anymore. What was his name?"

Emily smiled. "I knew your curiosity would get the best of you."

"True enough. So what was it?"

She leaned toward him and whispered in his ear. "*Cristos.*"

Mason considered it for a while, as serious as a monk. "That's a hell of a name."

"It's nice. And it suits him, don't you think?"

Mason looked as thoughtful as Emily had ever seen him. In a very serious voice he said, "Cristos and Sarita, sittin' in a tree, k-i-s-s-i-n-g."

Emily laughed and swatted him on the arm. "You are such a clown!"

"Sometimes." He pulled her down and rolled on top of her, where perhaps Cristos had once embraced Sarita, one hundred years in the past.

"I love you," Emily said, and kissed him.

Epilogue

With the smell of sea salt in the air, Emily closed the laptop and slid it into her bag. She looked down at her sandals, debating whether or not to slip them on. The sun dazzled the sky, and the warmth of the day convinced her that barefoot was the only way to go.

She hooked the sandals by their straps and walked across the sand.

The Atlantic was on its best behavior today, charming the tourists with its peace and utter blueness. White foam rolled against the shore. Emily wore a wide-brimmed hat, but she pushed it off and let it hang down her back. She wanted the sun on her face.

She also wanted the man who was crouched on the ocean's edge.

Mason didn't see her coming. The cuffs of his faded jeans were rolled up to his ankles, his feet revealed by the departing tide. Around him he'd gathered what that tide had left behind, sections of gnarled driftwood, each bent and contoured into an interesting shape. He'd started incorporating these into his woodwork, an element he never would have enjoyed in Colorado. Three weeks ago, he'd sold his first major piece, and two more quickly after that. It seemed that Native woodworkers were a novelty around here.

He didn't look up as she approached, just kept his

dark eyes on the sea. She often caught him doing that, staring across the ocean as if bewitched by it. She wondered how long it would be before he dragged her onto a boat and set out over the waves.

"If I stare any longer at that computer," Emily said, "I'm going to require a serious massage to get rid of the headache."

Mason picked up a length of driftwood and turned it over in his talented hands. "That can probably be arranged. As far as masseurs are concerned, my services come pretty cheap."

She knelt beside him. This morning on their way to the beach, he'd insisted that they stop by the post office so he could mail a three-hundred-dollar check to the Arbor Day Foundation. It was his way of making amends for the damage he'd caused at his former place of employment. His friend had recovered fully from the burns, and the police had turned to more pressing investigations, but this did nothing to assuage Mason's guilt. Ever since they'd left Rockerton, he'd been looking for redemption. He finally decided that planting trees would be the most appropriate way to find it.

"I just got an email from a man in Utah."

"Utah?"

"He read my article. He said a lot of nice things."

Her first major publication had been released ten days ago in *American Heritage*, detailing their discoveries. She'd translated and transcribed many of the letters between Sarita and her beloved Cristos Ramon Diaz Salazar—patriot of Spain.

"But he wasn't writing simply to say how great I am. Even though I am."

"I agree. You *am*. What did he want?"

"He's found strange symbols carved on a cliff."

"Strange symbols, huh?"

She nodded.

"Sounds right up your alley."

"*Our* alley. I couldn't have done it without you."

"I like sharing alleys with you. Check this one out." He showed her the driftwood. At one point it had resembled a branch, but the sea had spun it into an almost supernatural shape. "I guess both of us are intrigued by secrets trapped in wood."

"Two of a kind."

"Hey, I was wondering something. If an image carved in a tree is called a dendroglyph, what's it called when I make a message in the sand?"

"Good question. I'll have to look it up."

Mason used his finger to write his initials, then added hers as if he were a boy inscribing his crush in a schoolhouse desk: MH + ER.

That sentiment meant more than she could say. His simple, wild feelings for her came through in everything he did. She never wanted it to end.

"So when are we running off to Utah?"

"Later," she said as their lips touched.

"But not tonight?"

"Don't we have other plans tonight?"

"Only if they're the kind of plans we can do in the dark," he said.

"My favorite kind…"

The tide pushed up the shore, erasing the letters he'd written there.

Kissing him, Emily didn't care.

A word about the author...

Lance Hawvermale published his first novels under the female pseudonym of Erin O'Rourke. Since then, his poetry and fiction have garnered numerous awards. In 2016, St. Martin's Press released Hawvermale's fifth novel, *Face Blind*, a thriller set in Chile's Atacama Desert.

Hawvermale is an alumnus of AmeriCorps, performing his service on the Otoe-Missouria tribal lands in Red Rock, Oklahoma. He has worked as a college professor, an editor, and a youth counselor. He lives in Texas with his family and their cats.

Visit his website at www.lancehawvermale.com.

Thank you for purchasing
this publication of The Wild Rose Press, Inc.

For questions or more information
contact us at
info@thewildrosepress.com.

The Wild Rose Press, Inc.
www.thewildrosepress.com

To visit with authors of
The Wild Rose Press, Inc.
join our yahoo loop at
http://groups.yahoo.com/group/thewildrosepress/